BY THE SAME AUTHOR

Megan 1
Megan 2
Megan 3
Amy
Two Sides of the Story

and for younger readers:

BEST PETS SERIES
Gita and Goldie
Timmy and Tiger
Becky and Beauty
Paul and Percy

holly

mary hooper

BLOOMSBURY

First published in Great Britain in 2000
Bloomsbury Publishing Plc, 38 Soho Square, London, W1V 5DF

Copyright © Mary Hooper 2000

The moral right of the author has been asserted
A CIP catalogue record of this book is available from the
British Library

ISBN 0 7475 4863 3

Printed in Great Britain by Clays Ltd, St Ives plc

10 9 8 7 6

Thanks to my friends at
National Missing Persons Helpline

chapter one

I remember the day the first parcel arrived. I remember it because the brown paper package came with the rest of the post for the shop and then just sat on the shelf, waiting for someone to bother to take it downstairs to the office, which is next to the staffroom. And because Mrs Potter, who's the shop manager, didn't come in until late afternoon, it was only then that I found out it was for me. It was a dead boring day and the customers had been playing up something rotten, so I was a bit miffed – thinking that I could have had this exciting thing, this surprise parcel, to open and think and gloat about all day if only I'd known about it earlier.

As it was, the day was dominated by – well, tiresome customers, of course, but mostly by Ella's phone call. By midday she and I had had our lunch, which had been a sandwich from the Tempting Treats menu, and were sitting staring at the payphone in the staffroom downstairs from the shop.

'Oooh-er,' she wailed, 'I can't do it!'

'Go *on*!' I urged. 'You must. Now that you've got this far.'

'Oooh … what if he doesn't want to … I mean, what if they find him and he just says he's not interested in me?'

'He *will* be interested!' I said, pretending to sound certain.

She gave a squeal and clutched at her tummy. 'I don't know if I can.' She looked up at me and asked pathetically, 'Will you phone for me?'

I shook my head. 'Suppose they ask me something I don't know the answer to. Look – ' I took her hand – 'I'll hold your hand. I'll dial the number for you!'

'Go on, then.' She pushed the piece of paper towards me and I dialled the Freephone number and then gave her the receiver.

Ella made a strangled noise sounding like '*Help*!'

I didn't mind all this fuss because Ella's my best friend and anyway, it was quite exciting and something different to think about. It was the school summer holidays – we were both going back into Year 11 in September. Ella and I had temporary jobs in a big tea shop near where we live. Well, to be quite accurate, it was an Olde Tea Shoppe and a tourist trap. The town where we live is just outside London and it's got a palace with Henry VIII connections, so it gets a million visitors a year. Or it might be two million, I forget. Anyhow, there were a lot of tourists and as they were mostly American we called them doodles – from Yankee-doodles – and loads of them came into the tea shop, and there we were dressed all Olde Englishe in long blue check dresses and big white aprons, with soppy bits of hats stuck on our heads. We felt really stupid. Or we did at first, but in the end I kind of got used to looking like a cross between a nurse and a crinoline doll. At least the uniforms were kept at work, so we could change when we got there and didn't have to walk through the streets looking daft.

We were both pleased to have the jobs, as we were desperate for money for clothes and stuff. It wasn't all that brilliantly paid, but we got tips, sometimes really good ones from the Americans, who – because they were only in England for a couple of days – often didn't bother to work out the money and just gave us whatever came to hand, which was usually a pound coin or three. We usually worked Monday to Friday, because although the shop was open at the weekends there was a regular weekend staff that worked throughout the year.

That morning, as the phone rang on, Ella stared at me, terror written all over her face. It rang about five times, then I heard the person on the other end say, 'Missing Persons Helpline.'

Ella's eyes widened, but she didn't say anything.

I nudged her hard. 'Say something!'

'Can I help you?' the woman's voice asked. It sounded quite posh, but friendly and concerned as well. As if she really did want to help.

'I ... want ... ' Ella began falteringly.

I squeezed her hand encouragingly.

'Yes?' the voice asked.

'I want to contact my dad,' Ella said in a rush.

'And how long has he been missing?' I heard the voice say.

Ella made frantic eyes at me. 'Since I was two.'

'And how old are you now?'

Ella looked at me again and raised her eyebrows. She was ready for this one. 'Eighteen,' she lied. She knew that you had to be eighteen.

'And has there been any contact between you and your dad since he left home?'

Ella swallowed. 'No. At least, I don't know. My mum and dad are divorced and she always said that she'd burn anything that came from him. So … '

'All right. What's your name?' the voice asked kindly, and when Ella told her, said, 'Do you have any details about your dad? His date of birth, for instance?'

Ella stared down at the piece of paper she held. 'Eleventh September 1953.'

'And do you know anything else about him? Did he marry again after your mum and dad divorced?'

'I'm not sure … ' Slowly, Ella started giving the information, her voice sounding less strained and scratchy with every word. I knew she was pleased to be talking about her dad and telling someone about him.

Ella's mum had recently got married again, for the third time. The first husband, Ella's dad, had walked out on them (or been driven out, Ella always said), the second one had spent most of his time drunk, and the third one, this new one, Ella hated with a passion. He bossed her about and told tales to her mum about her and was altogether a complete pillock. I'd only met him a few times but I thought he was snidey. Once I went round there in a short skirt and he looked at me in a funny way and said something about little girls not wearing short skirts unless they meant it. I told my mum about him and she said I should take care not to be alone with him, not under any circumstances.

I couldn't understand Ella's mum marrying someone like that, but – well, she was a bit dodgy too, actually. She had hair that was bleached as white as straw, and was the only mum I knew who had a tattoo of a Harley-Davidson motorbike badge on her arm.

I knew that Ella desperately wanted to find her real dad. She'd been talking about him for ages but since her mum had married the pillock, as we usually called him, it had become really important to her. I know what she was hoping, of course: that he'd come and get her and take her away from her mum and the pillock, then she and her dad would live together happily ever after. It all sounded a bit fairy-tale to me, but I wasn't going to say so. And, well, he *might* come along, and he might have a big car and a beautiful house with an indoor swimming pool, like she dreamed about.

I listened as Ella gave her address to the woman at

the helpline. She then put the phone down and beamed at me. 'They're sending forms!' she said. 'They've put me on the database and are sending forms.'

'And then what?'

'I've got to fill them in, giving as many details as possible about where he came from and what he might be doing for a job, and then when I return the forms to them they'll start looking for him.'

I stood up and readjusted my mobcap thingy, because it was nearly time to go back to work. 'But that doesn't mean to say that they'll definitely find him, does it?'

Her face fell.

'I mean, I'm not being horrible but I don't think you should get your hopes up *too* much.'

'But if he knows that I'm looking for him! He must want to know about me.'

'Yes, but he might have … ' I paused. 'He might have got married again and have another family.'

She frowned. 'That's what the woman on the phone said. She told me he might have a new family now and that I might cause him embarrassment.' She brightened up a little. 'That's nothing, though, is it? He'll soon get over a bit of embarrassment. I mean, he'll have to. He must want to know about me. I *need* him. He's got to come and rescue me from pillock attack.'

I giggled.

'I bet he's nice,' she said wistfully. 'I bet he's really nice. One of them's got to be, haven't they? It's not fair if I have a mum and dad who're *both* horrible. I bet he's done all right for himself, too. I bet he lives in a decent house and not just some grotty old council flat.' She heaved a sigh. 'I wish I had your mum and dad!' she said, not for the first time.

I pulled a face. This wasn't to say that I didn't think I had a decent mum and dad – I did. It was just that I didn't want to gloat about them in front of Ella.

They were pretty OK, as it happened. I mean, we did have rows sometimes, but not terrible ones with yelling, ripping of clothes and throwing people down the stairs like they have in Ella's house. My mum's quite young for her age – she's fifty – not in the way Ella's mum's young, with tight jeans and dangling ear-rings, but just quite giggly and chatty. She's the sort of person who wants to know who's asked who out and whether there's been any snogging and all that. I don't always tell her about the snogging, mind you, especially if it's been me who's been doing it.

My dad's about six years older than her and he's OK, too, but in a different way. He's not giggly, and he's got a bit of a beer gut and he's balding, but he's quite good at sorting things: problems at school or bus timetables or homework. He's cuddly, too – and sensible and calm and quite different from my mum, who's a bit scatty.

'Have you told your mum you're looking for him?' I asked Ella.

She shook her head. 'I told her once before that I wanted to find him, and she said she didn't know why I was bothering. That he was a useless layabout.' She shrugged. 'She would say that, though.'

'Have you got any photos of him?'

She gave a short laugh. 'No, because she's got rid of them. There are some of the day they got married but she's cut him off. *She's* there in her long white dress holding on to thin air. She won't tell me anything about him – I expect she's forgotten because of all the others she's had since.'

In between the husbands, her mum had had a succession of boyfriends. Occasionally they'd moved in and sometimes there had been an extra child or two around that Ella had had to share her room with. I was just going to ask about the pillock's children when

Cody, who's the assistant manager, stuck his head round the door of the staffroom.

'Are you two still in here?' he asked.

'What's it look like?' Ella said. Not rudely, though, but in a funny way. Cody's only a few years older than us and he's all right. Not good-looking – although the striped cotton jackets and gingham bow ties all the guys who worked in the tea shop have to wear don't help.

'It looks like you're five minutes late,' he said. 'And I'll have less of your cheek. Get on that floor and get serving.'

We got. As we went up the stairs we left staffroom land of black plastic and peeling wallpaper and entered one which had pale-pink walls hung about with painted china plates, tiddly bits of brass, sparkly cut glass and big arrangements of artificial flowers. As we went up I glanced at the little pile of post and noticed the brown paper package again, though I can't really say why I did.

Mrs Potter came in at four thirty. She part-owns the shop and is really nice. She's about forty, I suppose, and she always wears a navy-blue suit with a check blouse instead of a dress and an apron. She waved hello to us as she passed through the tea room and went downstairs. About ten minutes later she came back, holding the package. She caught my eye as I cleared away some disgusting debris on a table for four – it looked as if they'd been dunking their almond tarts in their tea – and held it up.

'This is for you,' she said.

I didn't think I'd heard her properly. I finished putting the stuff on the tray and went up to her.

'For you,' she said again. 'It just says *Holly Devine c/o Ye Olde Tea Shoppe*, and on the other side it says, *Please see that she gets this. Thank you.* Very polite, who-ever it's from.' She put the package on a shelf on the other side of the counter. 'Open it when you've got a minute.' She added in a jolly voice, 'And let me know what it is, won't you?'

She went downstairs again and I dumped the tray in the kitchen and picked up the package.

It was addressed just as she'd said, and it felt squashy. I didn't recognise the writing. Ella came into the kitchen behind me. 'What's that?' she asked.

'A present from someone!' I said, though I didn't know if it was. It could have been a couple of old newspapers wrapped up, for all I knew. 'It was delivered here.'

'Ooh, get you!' she said. She gave the package a squeeze. 'Is it from Alex?'

Alex was the boy I was going out with. 'I shouldn't think so,' I said. 'That's not the sort of thing he'd do – send surprises through the post. Anyway, he'd have sent it to me at home.'

'Not if it's a pair of French knickers,' Ella said.

'I wish.' I tore at the package, which had sticky tape all round it. Inside there was dark-blue tissue paper, and inside this, a scarf. A beautiful scarf – lambswool, I thought. Very pale-blue, very soft.

'That's nice,' Ella said admiringly.

I held the scarf up, putting it against my face. A note fluttered to the ground and I bent and picked it up.

There was no address or signature. It just said:

Holly. I hope you won't mind me buying you this. I think it's the sort of thing you'll like. Am I right? And I think it matches your eyes. This comes with best wishes from (and I know it's corny) A Friend.

A pale-blue scarf. That's what started it all.

chapter two

'I t's beautiful. That's cashmere,' Mum said. She stroked her hand gently up and down the blue scarf. 'It's a pashmina.'

'What's that?'

She shrugged vaguely. 'It's just what they're called. They're from India or somewhere, and they use the best, softest yarn from the underside of some sort of goat. It cost a lot of money, I can tell you that.'

'How much?' I asked.

'About a hundred pounds, I should think.'

'Blimey!' I said, astounded.

We were in the kitchen, where Mum was painting terracotta pots in order to put moss balls in them and sell them at the school Christmas fair. It was months away but she always had a stall there and started making stuff around August or September.

'Pashmina,' I said. It sounded nice. 'Pash-me-na.' I looked at it. It seemed different now I knew it was expensive. Before it had been very nice, but it was just a scarf, something Mum might buy me on the spur of the moment if she was walking through Marks. Now it was a *pashmina*, though, from India or somewhere, it was different. And someone different from a mum had bought it for me. Someone who – let's not have any false modesty here – must fancy me to bits to spend so much money on me.

A rich doodle, then? But they were only passing through, so why would they bother to send a scarf to me? I tried to think whether we'd had anyone likely in the shop. Had I noticed anyone giving me the eye? I didn't *think* so. And surely if you were going to spend a lot of money and buy someone a *pashmina*, you'd want to make sure that that someone had noticed you by leaving them a big tip or engaging them in conversation or whatever. No one had done that.

Of course I'd seen, very occasionally, boys that I quite liked the look of – there had been a really gorgeous German boy a week or so back – but I only fancied the young, fairly scruffy student types. It couldn't be one of them. They'd never be able to afford a hundred pounds for a scarf.

'But of course you can't keep it,' Mum went on. She moved a silver-painted pot along the newspaper to join the others in the drying zone.

'Why not?'

'You can't just take presents from a complete stranger. He might be a bit dodgy – he's *bound* to be a bit dodgy. Who goes round giving presents to young girls they don't know? If you take this, he might expect something in return.'

'What – my body, you mean?'

'You can joke … '

'OK,' I said, 'but how am I supposed to give it back?'

She thought for a moment. 'I don't really know. It'll probably be from someone who's seen you in the shop – otherwise they'd know where you live and would have sent it here. So perhaps you ought to leave it in the shop and then if someone comes in … '

'Who looks a bit dodgy,' I finished, 'I could serve the scarf up with their pudding.'

'OK,' she said, 'if you're determined to make a joke of it, go ahead. But I'm serious. I think you ought to take care. Make sure you always leave and come home with Ella, won't you?'

I nodded vaguely, draping the pashmina around me and rubbing my nose into the softness of it. 'Does it?' I said.

'What?'

'Match my eyes?'

Mum laughed and looked at me, head on one side. 'Not bad,' she said. 'It matches three-quarters of your eyes.'

I have an odd eye – my right – which is half blue and half brown. I quite like having it. Sometimes I make my right eye up in blue and brown, half and half, hoping that people will notice it more, but they hardly ever do.

I put the scarf down. 'Guess what?' I said. 'Ella's trying to find her real dad.'

'Is she really?' Mum said. 'And what does her mother have to say about that?'

'She doesn't know.'

'Oh, dear,' Mum said. 'I see trouble ahead. I bet the new husband won't like it either.'

'He hates Ella,' I said. 'He's horrible to her. He might be quite pleased if her real dad came along one day and took her.'

'Ah, well,' Mum said, 'I hope he does in a way, because that girl's had a bit of a rough life, what with one thing and another.' She shook her head thought-fully. 'But then things don't always work out quite the way you expect.' She frowned and then she said, 'Should I do a few more gold ones, d'you think?'

I looked at the finished pots sitting in rows along the table. There were about ten of each, silver and gold. I shook my head. 'I don't like the gold ones so much.'

'Everyone else does, though,' Mum said, and she picked up the gold stuff she'd been using. 'Pass me that brush, darling.'

'I don't know why you asked me, then!' I draped my scarf, my pashmina, around my neck again. When Mum was painting it didn't do to leave things lying around. 'You don't think it's from Alex, do you?'

'He couldn't afford it!' Mum said. 'And quite honestly, love, he hasn't got the style.'

'You don't like him!' I said accusingly.

'I do, you know I do. But he wouldn't even *think* about buying someone a pashmina to match her eyes.'

'D'you really think it cost a hundred pounds?'

'Probably.' Another gold pot emerged and was moved to the drying area. 'Around that, I should think.'

I looked for a label. 'Think what I could buy for a hundred pounds! Maybe I can take it back.'

'Maybe you can *give* it back,' she said. 'I really don't like you accepting a present like that from someone we don't know.'

'Mmm. Maybe,' I said vaguely.

Dad came in and admired the scarf, and when Mum said it was from a secret admirer he looked startled.

'Secret admirers,' he said. 'At your age!'

'Of course.' I wrapped the scarf around my face, wondering if I looked like an exotic foreign spy. 'It's never too early to start having secret admirers.'

'So I see,' he said, and he poked me in the tummy in a playful way. But neither Mum nor I told him how much it was worth.

In my room later, I got ready to meet Alex. I wanted to wear the pashmina, although it was nowhere near cold enough. And really, to be quite honest, a pale-blue woolly scarf wasn't the sort of thing I would normally wear to go bowling. I looked in the wardrobe for something to go with it, though.

My wardrobe was a mess. I had no decent clothes – and come September it would really show, because there was no uniform in sixth form. That meant we would all be wearing our own stuff and, as I had absolutely nothing worth wearing, I was dreading it.

I wouldn't mind if I had my own style. Ella, for instance, dresses a bit tarty so she always knows what sort of thing to go for. There's another girl at school, Georgie, who's Goth (and doesn't seem to care that Goth went out ages ago), and two more who are kind of New Age or Gypsy, and a girl named Jasmine who wears everything oriental. It's fine for them, they've decided what sort of style they are, so even if they wear something that's not quite right, the *sense* of themselves that they've already established makes them look all right. Or at least that's what I think.

I'm quite tall and thin and I look OK in long, flowing things so I could get away with looking Gypsy, apart from being fair instead of having dark Romany colouring. But I knew I couldn't suddenly appear like that, transformed into Gypsy overnight as if I was born again. The two girls who're into that look have been wearing it since they were about twelve.

It would make it easier if I was going to a different school to take my A levels, somewhere where no one knew me. I could start there being someone quite different, then. I wasn't, though, so I had to stay ordinary. I ended up putting on jeans, of course, and an off-white T-shirt. Not exactly at the cutting edge.

When Alex knocked at the door, I hung the scarf

over my shoulder before I went to answer it. I figured that if the scarf was from him by some faint chance (they'd fallen off the back of a lorry, say), then he'd see it and start laughing.

He saw it and said, 'Got a stiff neck?'

I gave him a kiss on the cheek. 'D'you like it?'

He shrugged. 'It's all right. Why're you wearing it?'

'Someone sent it to me.'

'Who?' he asked.

We walked through to the garden. 'No idea,' I said airily. 'Just someone who fancies me, I suppose.'

'You must know,' he said.

'I don't!'

We went on like this for a while, until he got ratty and I began to realise that I shouldn't have hinted it was from a secret admirer. Alex just wasn't the sort of boy who could shrug this off.

'Look, I thought it might have been from you – that's the only reason I'm wearing it,' I said in the end.

He stared at me hard, his nose inches from mine. He was good-looking, dark, with thick, short hair that stood up in little points when it was gelled. 'Take it off, then,' he said.

'All right! Don't lose your rag about it. I don't even like it that much!' I lied. 'It's only some old scarf.'

Just then, Mum came into the garden and went towards the shed with a tray full of her pots. She beamed at us both. 'Seen the scarf, Alex?' she asked.

'Could hardly miss it,' he muttered.

'A mystery, eh? Someone with money to burn, though!'

I glowered at her. *Thanks, Mum.*

He waited until she'd offloaded the pots and gone in again, and then he said, 'I thought you said it was just some old scarf?' He fingered it, frowning deeply. 'Was it expensive? Is there something special about it?'

'Apparently,' I said. 'From an Indian goat's tummy or something – I don't know.' I tossed the scarf on to the garden seat as if I couldn't care less about it. 'Can't we just shut up about it now?'

Neither of us mentioned it after that but Alex was just a little bit miffed for the rest of the evening. His game was off, too – usually he beats everyone else hands down but that evening even *I* beat him.

chapter three

A few days later, Ella brought all the forms about finding her dad into the shop and during our lunchtime break I helped her fill them in.

The first questions were quite straightforward – his full name and date of birth, and Ella had these. The next question asked if he was named on her birth certificate, and said that if he wasn't, then they wouldn't be able to help.

'Is he?' I asked.

She nodded. 'Course he is. He was married to my mum then.'

We went down the form. She couldn't give any description to speak of, though she thought her dad had been quite tall, because she could just remember someone looming over her in her pushchair. I said that anyone would loom when you were small enough to be in a pushchair and she said she was positive he was tall and slim and distinguished-looking. (The pillock, by the way, is fat and squatty and wears shell suits.)

The form asked when she'd last seen him, and under what circumstances they'd parted, then wanted to know what sort of job he'd done. At the bottom of the page it asked if she would agree to publicity.

I pointed this out. 'Do you?' I asked. 'D'you want his name given out on one of those *Missing* programmes on TV?'

'Course I do,' she said.

'But what will your mum say when she finds out you're looking for him? And suppose he doesn't like being named on TV? Suppose it scares him off?'

She stared at me. 'But he won't be scared off! He'll be pleased to be back in touch with me. He'll be pleased I found him!'

Her eyes had filled with tears, so I hastily agreed with her. 'Yeah, I expect he will,' I said.

She took a deep breath. 'I've got to write him a letter.'

'What for?'

'In case they find him. If they do find him, they

send him a letter and see if he wants to be in touch.' She waved the leaflet which had come with the forms. 'They don't let me know his address unless he gives permission.'

'I shouldn't write too much,' I said cautiously. I knew what Ella was like. If left unchecked she'd write pages and pages, pouring out all her hopes, fears, and complaints about the pillock, etc. She'd probably end up saying that she wanted to live with him and his new family. 'You want to take it gently. Don't frighten him off by saying you want him to rescue you or anything.'

'What shall I say, then?' she asked. 'You're better at that sort of thing than I am.'

We got a pad to practise on, and after three goes, this is what she wrote.

Hello, Dad!
I expect you'll be surprised to hear from me, but I've been dying to find you again for years. I know lots has happened since you were living with Mum, but I still think about you all the time.

I am getting on quite well at school and will be going into sixth form to take my A levels next year.

I have lots and lots to tell you. Please get in touch.

Whatever has happened, you are still my dad and I really want to see you.

All my love,
Ella

'Is that enough?' she said anxiously. 'Are you sure that's all right?'

'It's perfect,' I assured her.

She put it in her bag to post on the way home and we went upstairs to start on a coach party's clotted-cream teas (two scones each, one miniature jar of jam, one small dish of cream and a pot of tea).

It was about four o'clock that the flowers arrived. I was clearing a table and pocketing a pound tip when I saw the florist's van stop outside. I didn't take much notice until the driver got out and came towards the shop carrying something dark-green and purple.

I was nearest the door and opened it. He handed over the bunch of flowers and said, 'These are for Holly Devine.'

'That's me,' I said, astonished.

'There you go, then!' he said, grinned and went off.

I stood there holding them while all the customers

goggled at me and Mrs Potter beamed and nodded from behind the cash till.

Ella rushed over. 'Ooh, what've you got now?'

Red as a beetroot, I put the flowers on the tray with the dirty crockery and carried the whole lot through to the kitchen.

Then I looked at them properly.

The flowers were anemones, blue and purple, tightly packed and surrounded by shiny green holly – the sort without any prickles. Around the whole bunch was a big, shimmering sheet of cellophane paper, and it had been wrapped so that the bottom of the cellophane was shaped into a vase and contained real water.

'Where's the note? Where's the note?' Ella said, staring at the flowers in envy.

I shook my head. 'I don't think there is one.'

'Holly for Holly!' she said unnecessarily, pointing to the greenery.

'I know,' I said. They weren't just any old bunch of flowers. They'd been chosen, and the bunch had been made up, specially for me. I'd never had a bunch of flowers given to me before. Let alone delivered by a van.

Mrs Potter had left the till and followed me into

the kitchen. 'How exquisite!' she said. 'D'you know who they're from?'

I shook my head.

'The same person that sent the scarf!' Ella said. 'Must be.'

'I suppose so,' I said.

My cheeks were still flaming, and to try and hide them I bent over the bunch again, pretending to look for a note. A damp, flowery smell came up to me and I sniffed deeply. Flowers, specially for me! Gorgeous flowers, not some naff old carnations bought from a garage or anything (Ella had once had those) but stylish, tasteful flowers.

'And haven't you any idea who they're from?' Mrs Potter marvelled. 'Is it your birthday or anything?'

I shook my head.

'Just think ... it might be one of our customers.' She looked out into the tea room, where a dozen men of assorted ages, shapes and sizes waited for their tuna baguettes or their egg-mayonnaise rolls. It had been raining for a while and they all looked damp, dishevelled, old – and highly unlikely to have sent me something so gorgeous. At least, I really hoped they were unlikely.

Stacey and Mandy, the other waitresses, had come

into the kitchen now and were staring at the flowers, and the two women who worked in the kitchen stopped buttering bread and were staring too and saying, 'Ooh, got a secret admirer, then?' and 'Someone means business and no mistake.'

'Did you see where the van came from?' Ella asked. 'We could go in there and ask who sent them!'

Mrs Potter, suddenly realising that most of the shop staff were crowded into the kitchen, clapped her hands. 'Come on! You can discuss it during your break, girls,' she said. 'There are half a dozen tables waiting for orders.'

I put my flowers carefully on a side shelf and went back to finish clearing my table. The rest of the afternoon, though, every time I had to go up to that end of the shop I glanced in at them, sitting there in all their purple and blue loveliness.

At five thirty we turned the sign on the door to say *Closed* and tried to hurry out those customers who were still sitting around by swishing a damp cloth over their tables and over them too, if they didn't move fast enough. I cleared the dead crockery on my section and hurried downstairs to change. I wanted to get my flowers home and gloat over them.

*

'So did you notice the name on the van that brought them?' Mum said, examining the flowers carefully and marvelling over them in just the right way.

'I didn't,' I said, 'but Stacey said it was from the place up by the station. I went there on the way home but they were closed.'

'Hmm,' Mum said. 'They're gorgeous – but I don't like it.'

'Why not?'

'I just don't like the idea of you getting presents from someone you don't know. There are some dodgy people around these days. I've a good mind to come up in the afternoons and meet you.'

'Mum!' I said. 'Don't you dare!'

She looked at me and frowned. 'It might be some-one who thinks you're a lot older than you are. With your hair up like that, you look at least eighteen.'

I picked up the flowers and was just about to take them upstairs to my room so I could look at them and think about who might have sent them, when we heard Dad's key in the lock.

'See what Dad thinks,' Mum said.

Dad came into the kitchen, yawning and looking tired, but he grinned when he saw Mum and me with our heads together. 'What are you two up to?' he said.

'Looks like a conspiracy. Looks like I've got to go trailing round the shops tomorrow.'

I was a bit worried when I saw that smile – worried because for a split second I thought *he* might have sent the flowers and the pashmina. He'd sent me a Valentine card once, when I was about eleven. It had been a Saturday and Ella had rung me, hysterical with excitement, to say that a huge card with a silver heart had just arrived for her. I'd hardly thought about boys up till then – let alone Valentine cards – but when Ella had rung to tell me she'd got one, I suddenly, desperately, wanted one too.

Later I'd gone shopping with Mum and Dad and when we got back, there was the Valentine card, lying on the mat. It was a cheap and flimsy one, though, and I knew immediately and miserably that it had been bought from the Eight Till Late shop at the end of the road. Dad never, ever, owned up to sending it, mind you, but he didn't have to.

The split second came and went, though, as I realised that he wouldn't ever have sent me two such expensive things. He wasn't tight, but he'd never splash his money around on things like that without good reason, even for me.

I showed him the flowers and then went through

all the stuff with him that I'd just been through with Mum ('Really ought to be careful … must be up to no good … can't take any chances in this day and age,' etc.) and in the end I had to promise that I would take *enormous* care and always come home from the tea shop with Ella and never talk to strangers or anything like that.

Afterwards, I carried the flowers off to my bedroom and stared at them for about half an hour, wondering and dreaming a bit. Suppose they were from someone rich, young and gorgeous? And maybe he was rich because he was famous in some way – with one of the bands? But no, it couldn't be that, because if anyone halfway famous, a singer or anyone, had come into the shop, we'd have noticed him. Anyway, even if it was someone fanciable, what was I supposed to do about it? I was going out with Alex, I couldn't just dump him. Well, not unless this unknown someone was just too entirely wonderful and irresistible and swept me off my feet and wanted to take me to Venice. Whoever had sent the things was surely going to be someone interesting, and naturally I was going to look at every single man who came in the tea shop from now on: old, young, fanciable, frumpy – they were *all* going to be carefully scrutinised.

*

The next day, before work, Ella and I, giggling madly, called in at the station florists. I explained that I worked in Ye Olde Tea Shoppe and about the flowers and everything.

The woman looked on her computer screen and then shook her head. 'I'm afraid the order was placed at another branch,' she said. 'All I had to do was carry out the instructions given.'

'Which other branch, though?' I asked.

The woman shrugged. 'There's no way of telling. The shop that the buyer called at contacted our central service line over the Internet.'

'So could I ring this central line?' I asked. 'Maybe they'll remember his name.'

The woman shook her head. 'It's all computerised. He might have ordered them on a credit card from our website and that's just impossible to trace. Anyway – ' she smiled – 'it might not have been a *he*.'

Ella nudged me. 'Whooo!'

'Don't be daft,' I said. I wasn't going to have it that my secret admirer was a woman. Anything but that. No, he was young, male, rich, gorgeous – and probably a film star.

chapter four

'Is there any news about my dad yet?' Ella asked. It was lunchtime the following Monday and we were in the staffroom on the telephone. Ella's head was tilted to one side and the receiver was angled so that I could listen in, too. 'Have you found out anything?'

'I'm really sorry,' the woman at the helpline said. Her name was Maureen and she was, she'd told Ella, her case manager. 'We've only just started making our enquiries and it'll be some time before we hear back.' There was a pause. 'I see when you filled in the form, you said you were going to try and find out some further information about other members of the family, and what sort of job your dad might be doing.'

'I haven't found out anything,' Ella muttered. 'Sorry.'

She'd tried – I knew she had. She'd asked her mum if her dad had had any brothers and sisters and in the middle of it the pillock had come in. He'd wanted to know what Ella was asking about 'that loser' for, and said that if he (real dad) had wanted her he would have come back for her, but judging by the state of *her* it was no surprise he hadn't.

Poor old Ella had got really upset and – this amazed me, though it shouldn't have really because I knew what her mum was like – she had sided with the pillock and it had all ended up in a flaming row.

'When he lived with my mum, he used to be a car mechanic,' Ella said now. 'But I don't know if he's still doing it.'

'Any information helps,' said the woman. 'Perhaps he's working at a garage or car showroom or something.'

'So how long d'you think it will take?' Ella asked.

'It's difficult to say. And you mustn't build your hopes on it, Ella,' the voice went on kindly. 'Even if we can get a letter to him, he might not reply. He might have decided to make a new life for himself. Lots of people do, you know. They cut themselves off and then find it too difficult to start having contact again.'

Ella turned to look at me, big tears welling up in her eyes.

'But you can ring me any time you like,' the voice said, 'even if you just want to chat about things.'

Ella made a gulping noise in her throat and I knew she couldn't speak because she was too choked. The woman must have known that, too. 'I'll tell you what,' she said. 'If you like, I'll put him on our Missing page for a week.'

'What's that?' Ella asked.

'It's on Teletext. We've got our own Missing page and we put about twenty names on at a time. It's very low-key publicity – no photo or anything – just his name and a few brief details about him.'

'Oh, yes please,' Ella said.

'Look out for it next week, then.'

The woman told her the page number and said that they'd be in touch immediately if they heard anything.

The tears had gone and Ella was beaming when she put the phone down. 'D'you hear that? He's going on telly. His name's going on telly!'

'Your mum will go spare!'

'Let her! On Monday for a week! He'll see it – I know he'll see it, and then he'll get in touch with me.'

I looked at my watch, we adjusted the silly white hats and we went out to serve the doodles. Working in the tea shop had got much more interesting for me since the pashmina and the flowers had arrived. It had given things a bit of an edge thinking there was a chance that someone came in there who fancied me. I'd taken to wearing make-up every day – I hadn't always bothered before then – and, after my mum's comment about my hair, nearly always had it up so that I looked older.

I practised being charming, too. Charming to every man who came in, because who knew *who* it might be? Even if it wasn't someone young and gorgeous, I liked the idea of getting surprises and quite fancied getting more. If the person hadn't declared himself by September when we had to go back to school, I wondered if the presents would start arriving there. *That* would increase my cred. I wouldn't even have to bother to think up a new, more interesting persona for myself, I'd be known as that girl who had a mystery admirer and presents arriving all the time.

*

Late that morning, an envelope arrived in the second post. It contained one of those small handmade cards: silver wire twisted into a little mouse shape on a background of a painted rainbow, very pretty. Inside, each one wrapped in a screw of tissue paper, was a pair of earrings, long, silver, with a tiny stone at the end of each one which Mrs Potter said was a moonstone. There was a note, too. In the same handwriting that had been on the first note, written with an ink pen in nice italic script. It said:

Would you like to meet? I want you to know I have only the best of intentions towards you, so would you like to bring your Mom or your best friend or someone? I suggest next Sunday, you say a time and place. You can leave a message on 07204-609654.

'Oh, wow!' Ella said as we stared at it. 'Can I come?'

'Course you can,' I said.

'That looks like a mobile number,' Ella said. 'And look how he's spelled *Mum* - with an 'o'. Like the Americans do.'

'Oh, yes,' I said. I nibbled at my bottom lip. I was thrilled at the thought of meeting him, of course,

43

but also a bit deflated and a bit worried. All the time he was a mystery admirer it was just that – a mystery. He could be anyone and I was free to make him an Eastern prince, a road protester or a Hollywood talent spotter, as the mood took me. Once I'd met him, though, all that would be over. I was scared he'd just turn out to be a quite boringly ordinary bloke.

At six fifteen that afternoon as I came down the road from work, Mum drove up in the car with a load of shopping. We carried everything indoors and, as she unpacked the stuff in the kitchen, I danced around wearing my new earrings and reading the card out to her.

'Look, aren't they lovely? I can go, can't I? What d'you think he'll be like?'

She frowned, picked up the card and examined the writing. Then she examined the earrings and shook her head. 'Expensive again,' she muttered. 'What's going on?'

'Well, we can find out now!' I said. 'I can go, can't I? Ella says she'll come with me. She's desperate.'

'I'm not letting you go with her!' Mum said. 'If you go at all, I'm going with you.'

I groaned. 'Do you have to? I'll be perfectly all right.'

'Don't look at me like that! As if I'd let you two go

44

on your own – you'd get kidnapped or something.'

'Mum! We're not ten years old!'

'I want to go with you and sort this out,' she said. 'I'm not having someone I don't know send you expensive presents. What's his game?'

I sighed. I'd guessed this was coming, of course. Guessed she wasn't going to let me go with Ella.

She banged tins into the top cupboard. 'I'll come with you and we'll take the presents back and say thank you but you can't possibly take any more expensive things from a stranger.'

I gave a great groan. 'Oh, no!' No more presents! And to have to give back those that I'd got! I began to wish I hadn't told her.

She turned from the cupboard. She had that uncanny ability that mums sometimes have of knowing what I was thinking almost before I did. 'Look, Holly, I know you needn't have told me about this, but I'm extremely pleased that you did. You must allow me to know the right thing to do, though. You don't know with these men – you're a lovely young girl and some men are dangerous.'

I tutted, swinging my head from side to side so that I could feel the cold stone of the earrings gently touching each cheek.

'You've heard of stalkers, haven't you? What about that woman who was killed last year by a stalker who'd been pursuing her for ten years?'

'This isn't like that,' I muttered. I didn't want to think that my secret admirer, my strikingly attractive band member, the person who'd sent such lovely things to me, was anyone horrible like a *stalker*.

'You can scoff, but if he's on the level, why doesn't he just turn up at the door in the normal way? Why all this secrecy business?'

'Dunno.' I shrugged.

'I'll ring him and give him a time and place,' she said decisively. She scrunched up the shopping bags and shoved them into a drawer. 'And I bet he doesn't turn up once he knows *I'm* coming.'

'Mum!' I protested again. 'Let me ring him. The card was for me. It said for *me* to ring.'

A bit of a battle ensued, with me saying that if she didn't let me ring I was never going to tell her if he contacted me again, and her saying that while I lived in this house under her roof I had to be guided by her, etc. It didn't go on for long, though – our rows never did. It ended with us deciding between us that I was allowed to ring him with a message arranged beforehand, while she listened in.

We then had to decide where we were going to meet. Mum said it ought to be somewhere out in the open and crowded. 'It's got to be somewhere we can just politely say our piece and then depart.'

'Suppose we don't want to depart?' I said. I couldn't help wondering whether he'd bring another present with him – something too big to post. 'We ought to hear him out. Suppose he's young and really nice? Suppose you like him, *approve* of him?'

'Suppose I don't,' she sniffed.

We decided to make the meeting place outside the gates of the old royal palace, near where we lived, at three o'clock the following Sunday. Although we could walk there, Mum said we should drive in case we wanted a quick getaway. After that, jittery with excitement, I rang the number he'd given. I was really quite nervous that he'd pick up the phone – that would have thrown me completely because I'd only rehearsed saying the place and time parrot-fashion. I wasn't ready to talk to him.

We went out into the hall to the telephone, with Mum squashed against me as close as she could possibly get.

He spoke quite quietly, and it was impossible to tell how old he was. He had a nice, deep voice and a faint accent which might have been Australian. He just said the number and 'Hi, I'm out. Please do leave me a message, though.'

I said, 'This is Holly. My mum and I would like to meet you on Sunday afternoon. Outside the old palace gates at three o'clock. Goodbye.'

'I couldn't hear his voice!' Mum said as I replaced the receiver. 'I wanted to hear how he sounded.'

'He hardly said anything.'

'Did he sound respectable?'

''Spose so. He didn't sound rough. He might be Australian.'

Australian didn't go with my daydreaming, somehow. Australian conjured up a picture of someone wearing one of those silly hats, or a surfing beach bum with bleached yellow hair. It would be OK if he was from one of the Aussie soaps, of course, but I didn't want a lager-swilling loser.

When I went back to my bedroom to have another little bit of a daydream, I picked up the card again and remembered Ella had mentioned that he'd written 'mom' in the note. So maybe he was American and not Australian. That would be better.

Well, whatever he was, in five days' time I was going to find out.

chapter five

'Y̲ou're going to meet him!' Alex said, sounding all gruff down the telephone line. 'What the hell are you doing that for? How would you like it if some girl was sending me stuff and I went off and met her?'

'It's not like a *date*,' I said. 'It's to give him his things back. Anyway, Mum's coming with me.'

It was Sunday morning. I hadn't told Alex about the meeting before, because I'd known he wouldn't like it. I'd had to tell him in the end, though, because he'd rung to ask me to go to the cinema that afternoon.

'It won't take long. I'll probably be back at half past three,' I said. 'I'll ring you as soon as I get in and we can go to the second show.'

As I spoke, I thought to myself that I'd be back at three thirty ... unless I met Mr Secret Admirer and fell madly in love with him, and then who knew when I'd be back?

I wasn't madly in love with Alex, that was a cert. I really liked him, but he was just a boy I went out with sometimes. I thought perhaps the madly-in-love bit might happen later, but Ella, who was a bit of an expert on these things, told me that it always happened at the beginning, and if it wasn't there then, then it never would be. Everything else was there, though: Alex was good-looking, funny, nice to me and didn't spend all night chatting to his mates when we were out together, so it was a bit of a disappointment that I wasn't soppy about him, but there you go. Anyway, I knew the soppiness didn't ever last: Mum had told me that it gradually gave way to what she called 'a nice companionship'. Who wanted to start off with a nice companionship, though? That was for when you were old. Sooner or later I wanted to sample the can't-eat-can't-sleep bit.

'And you're going to tell him to get lost, are you?' Alex said.

'Yeah. Sort of,' I said. 'At least, Mum is.'

'And you'll give him back his stuff?'

'Yes, yes,' I said, beginning to lose patience. 'Look, he's just going to be some weird old bloke, isn't he?' As I said it, I crossed my fingers and hoped madly that he wasn't. 'So when we get in, I'll ring you, right?'

'OK,' he said.

I'd only just put the phone down when it rang again and it was Ella.

'Guess what? He's on!' she said in a stage whisper.

'Who is?'

'My dad. On Teletext. I've been looking every day and it came on this morning. I nearly dropped dead when I saw his name there.'

'What's it say?'

'Go and look,' she said. 'Ooh, it really made me feel funny – seeing it written up in black and white.'

'Has your mum seen it?'

'No. No reason why she should. She never looks at Teletext. I don't suppose she knows what it is.' She sighed. 'I wonder if he'll see it. Or if someone else will see it and tell him about it.'

There was a long pause and then, just to bring the conversation round to me, I said, 'I'm getting ready to go in a minute.'

'Already! I thought you weren't meeting him until three o'clock?'

'Well, I want to look my best, don't I?' I said. 'He might have a present for me. I might be dripping in gold when I come back.'

'Huh!' she said. 'Ring me, won't you?'

'Course I will.'

'And go and look at my dad's name.'

I went into the sitting room and tapped out the number. National Missing Persons Helpline, it said at the top of the page, and then the pages turned over and there were lots of people missing: old, young, brothers, sisters, mothers, fathers, sons and daughters, all with their details and descriptions. Underneath it said things like, 'We're desperately worried', 'Left home after a family row' or 'Just ring home and let us know you're all right.'

Ella's dad was about the tenth one on, and I presssed HOLD when it got to him. It said:

Does anyone know the whereabouts of David Sullivan?

Little is known of his present appearance, but David is forty-six years old, used to live in the South-East, and may possibly be working as a car mechanic.

A member of his family would very much like to be in touch with him again and asks him to make contact through us.

Dad came in when I was looking at it.

'Look – it's Ella's dad!' I said. 'She's advertising for him.'

He read it carefully. 'But why doesn't it mention Ella as being the one who's looking for him?'

'In case he's got another family and hasn't told his wife he's been married before,' I said. 'They told Ella they always put that.'

'Oh dear, oh dear,' he said. 'Family break-ups. I don't know … ' Then he said, 'I think you'd better take my mobile phone this afternoon.'

I turned off the TV. 'What for?'

'So if there's any difficulty you can ring me. I'll be sitting here waiting and if necessary I can jump in the car and come to your rescue.'

'Like Batman?'

Dad nodded and grinned. 'Something like that. You just don't know who's going to turn up, do you? These young lads get – well – obsessive sometimes.' He put his arm round my shoulders and gave me a hug. 'I know I'm being an old stooge but I'd just feel better knowing you had the phone with you.'

'OK!' I said. Whatever. I was dying to meet this guy, whoever he was and whatever he was like. The nearer it got to three o'clock, the more excited I got.

*

At a quarter to three, Dad waved us off from the window, making a dialling-up motion with his hands. We nodded to him and waved back.

'You look nice,' Mum said as we drove down the road.

I shrugged. 'I thought I ought to make an effort.'

She glanced at me quickly again. 'You've got the earrings on. Take them off!'

I sighed. 'I thought I was just giving the scarf back.'

'*And* the earrings.'

'OK,' I said sulkily. I took them off and held them in my hand, which felt sticky with sweat. It was a blistering day and I kept coming over in great swoops of hotness. Who was he? What did he want? What if he was gorgeous?

'We'll go past the gates and into the proper car park,' Mum said, pausing at the traffic lights.

'It's two pounds an hour!'

'Never mind. We'll push the boat out.'

'How will we know him?'

'He'll know us, won't he? He'll know you, any rate. We'll just have to wait for him to approach us.'

I wiped my free hand on my skirt, looking out of the window at the crowds coming up the main road from the station. A hot summer Sunday always brought out the masses, some carrying picnic baskets and cool boxes, some pushing babies in pushchairs, some – the doodles – with maps, leather rucksacks and books on Henry VIII under their arms. The tea shop would be heaving.

We were almost up to the gate of the old palace, which was set back on cobbled stones with a man in a sentry box at each side. Mum stopped at the crossing just before the turning for the car park, and I leaned forward eagerly, undoing my seat belt in readiness. I couldn't see anyone gorgeous, but maybe he hadn't arrived yet. It was difficult to tell because there were so many people milling around.

'Anyone likely?' Mum asked, looking in her mirror. She indicated that she was about to turn into the car park.

'Not really,' I said, craning to see.

With the indicator blinking, we waited for a gap in the traffic and then began to drive in slowly. Mum glanced across at the people waiting in front of the gate and she suddenly seemed to stiffen slightly. I looked at her and was astonished to see she'd gone bone white.

'What's up?' I asked.

She opened her mouth and shut it again. She

carried on driving into the car park and went right past the attendant's box without stopping to pay.

'You're supposed to take a ticket!' I said, as the man waved at us.

'I wonder … ' She made a strange choking noise in her throat. She still looked very pale and almost ill. 'You know, I don't think this is such a good idea, Holly.'

'*What*?!'

'I've just got a sudden feeling about it – that it wouldn't be right, somehow. We don't know *who* we're going to meet. It could be very dodgy.'

'But you're with me. We've got the phone and everything. Look at all the people around. Nothing could happen to us!'

The car-park man arrived next to the car and tapped on the window. 'Afternoon, madam,' he said. 'May I give you a ticket?'

She didn't wind down the window, didn't even seem to see him there.

'I've got a bad feeling about it and I always take notice of my bad feelings,' she said. 'I don't think we should have come. You must leave another message saying that you never want him to contact you again.'

I looked at her in astonishment. 'But why?' I said.

'Why come all this way and then change your mind?'

'I told you. I just got a bad feeling.' She suddenly seemed to notice the car-park man and wound down her window. 'Sorry,' she said. 'We won't be stopping after all.'

'Please yourself, madam,' he said.

'But I want to meet him!' I said. 'I want to know what it's all about.' I put a hand on the door handle to open it and get out, but she leaned over and grasped it.

'Please,' she said. 'Please. I know I can't stop you but I really, really don't want you to go.' She sounded almost tearful and, stunned, I let my hand drop from the door handle.

'Just take my word for it. I've never let you down before, have I?'

I shook my head wordlessly.

'So trust me. I've got experience of the world. I know more about some things than you do.'

I didn't say anything, just looked at her. The colour was beginning to come back into her face now, but her eyes were all glassy and shocked. She looked as if she'd seen a ghost or had had some sort of psychic experience.

She hadn't turned off the car engine, and she just

glanced into the rear mirror and moved off. The exit was in a different place from the entrance and we drove across to it in silence. When she came out on to the main road she went right round the block, so that we didn't pass the old palace gates again, where we'd been supposed to meet him.

'I want you to ring and say you couldn't make it and won't be meeting him after all,' she said. 'Will you? Promise?'

'OK,' I said, but I crossed my fingers.

I was going to ring all right – but I wasn't going to say *that*.

chapter six

'Look, I'm really sorry if you were waiting there all afternoon,' I blurted out when he'd given his message and the answerphone had cut in. 'You see, we went along but my mum suddenly changed her mind about meeting you. Went all peculiar.' As I said this, I felt guilty, as if I was criticising her. 'Mums are a bit funny like that,' I added.

The answerphone, of course, gave no reply. Beside me, Ella nodded, encouraging me to go on with the next bit.

'I could meet you next weekend. Same time, same place,' I said. 'And this time I'll definitely be there. I'm going to bring my friend Ella with me.'

I wasn't, really, because she was going out with her auntie to a craft fair that day. I thought it was best to pretend this, though, just in case he thought I was coming on my own and started preparing to kidnap me.

'So, well. Sorry again. Goodbye,' I finished. I put the phone down and made an oh-my-gawd face at Ella.

'Your mum will positively kill you,' she said with satisfaction.

'She won't find out,' I said. 'I'm not going to say a word about it, and I'm going to tell her I'm going out with you to that craft fair, OK?'

Ella nodded. 'Suppose he gives you something else? Another present.'

I thought for a moment. 'If she sees it I'll pretend I bought it from the craft fair.'

'Suppose it's really expensive?'

I frowned. 'I *won* it in a competition at the craft fair,' I said after a moment.

'Oh, wow,' she said admiringly. 'Creative thinking.'

I felt bad about Mum really. If she found out I was going behind her back, she might not kill me, but she'd be bitterly disappointed in me. It might spoil our whole relationship. But even knowing that, I still had to go.

When I got home from work on Monday night

she'd asked me straight away if I'd rung him, and I said I had. She'd been quite intent on knowing whether he'd actually been there himself to answer the phone, but when I'd assured her, quite truthfully, that it had just been an answerphone again, she'd seemed to calm down a bit. I honestly don't think it occurred to her that I'd disobey her and arrange to go and meet him on my own. I'd never done anything like that before, never gone behind her back.

Alex, of course, had been pleased Mum and I hadn't actually met him. He'd said that Mum had done the right thing: the bloke was probably some sort of nutter and why had I wanted to meet him anyway? So I wasn't going to tell Alex that I was going, either.

The only person who knew the truth was Ella.

The week was hectic: more doodles, more trade, more cream teas. I didn't hear anything from *him* at all. I even wondered whether he'd got hacked off waiting last Sunday and had decided to call it a day. I went on being charming to everyone, of course, and wore make-up and washed my hair every two days, just in case. No customers gave me especially linger-ing looks over their prawn-and-mayo sandwiches, though.

For the first three days that week, Ella rang the Missing Persons Helpline every lunchtime, asking if anyone had seen her dad on Teletext and phoned in. On Wednesday her case manager, Maureen, said (very gently, I heard her) that it really wasn't worth ringing in every day because if they did hear anything, any news at all, they'd contact her straight away. Also for the first three days of that week, Mum asked me if I'd heard anything or got any more deliveries of presents. I said, again quite truthfully, that I hadn't.

I made sure Ella knew the time and venue for the meeting on Sunday and I arranged to ring her that evening at six, when she'd be back from the craft fair. I said I'd call anyway – whether I was back home or (just in case he was gorgeous) had gone off on a proper date somewhere. If I didn't ring her by six thirty, we joked, then I'd definitely been kidnapped and she'd let my mum and dad know straight away.

We laughed about it, but something inside me quivered whenever I said the word 'kidnapped'. Sometimes, lying in bed at night, I stopped seeing him as gorgeous and instead saw a shadowy figure bundling me, blindfolded, into the boot of a car, with a gag in my mouth so tight that I could hardly breathe. Whenever that happened, though, I told myself I'd been watching too many TV crime shows.

No, what I really really thought in the cold light of day was that I'd go off and meet this guy, but he'd be utterly boring and plain. Perfectly nice but with jeans from Woolworth's and he probably had spots. He'd say his piece and I'd say thank you, I was very flattered but unfortunately I already had a boyfriend. He'd then go off, sadly but with no hard feelings, into the sunset. It would be nice if I received the occasional bunch of flowers from him afterwards, but I'd understand if I didn't.

Sunday came. I was fiddling around, trying to do myself up a bit without it looking as if I was, when Mum said, 'Where's this craft fair you're going to?'

'At the community centre,' I said. I'd found this out, of course.

'I wouldn't mind a look in myself,' she said. 'Just to see if anyone's got any good ideas I haven't heard of yet.' She had, I knew, finished the moss-ball trees and had started on making sheets of home-made paper with bits of leaf stuck on them.

'Oh, OK,' I said. I spoke casually. *Oh, no, please don't!*

'You can't,' Dad said. 'I said we'd pop over and see my mum and dad this afternoon. The lawn's getting out of hand and I promised him I'd have a go at it.'

'Oh, all right, then,' Mum said. She turned back to me. 'Have a look for me, love, will you? See if there's anything new I might like doing.'

I nodded, breathed out and carried on getting ready.

'Ella coming round here for you, then?'

'No. I'm going there,' I said. 'And I might go and see a film with her later.' This bit might be true: if the day turned out to be a complete washout for whatever reason, then we'd said we'd go and see the new Brad Pitt. 'I'll give you a ring if I'm going to be late. Put my dinner on a plate and I'll microwave it.'

'OK, darling.' Mum smiled at me and reached for her handbag. 'Have a good time. Here's a fiver. Buy some earrings or something when you're there.'

I flushed guiltily, but years of taking from her made it quite easy to pocket the fiver. 'Cheers, Mum!' I said, turning away quickly and putting the money in my purse.

Mum and Dad had gone out by the time I left the house, which was a relief. While I'd been getting ready I realised that I should have arranged to meet him at a different time from last week. If she'd known I was going out at quarter to three, she might have caught on.

I looked at myself in the mirror on the way out and thought I looked fairly OK; I was a bit tanned, my hair had a couple of blond streaks from the sun and some freckles had come out across my nose. I was wearing my long denim skirt and a white top and had my leather rucksack with me, with the pashmina and earrings inside. I couldn't decide whether to give them back or not, and thought I'd just see how things went. I didn't want to lose them – who knew when someone might buy me something as expensive again? Besides, if I gave them back, what was I going to tell Mum when she asked about them?

I set off feeling fine, but was absolutely *dying* by the time I got to the old palace gates. Dying of fear, dying of embarrassment, dying of squirminess – you name it, I was dying of it. As I approached the meeting place, my legs were wobbly and my stomach was churning round like a washing machine.

I had a quick look round – no one to get excited about – and positioned myself by the wrought-iron gates, quite near to one of the little sentry-box things where the uniformed men sit. If necessary, I thought, I could dive into that sentry box and ask the man to save me.

It was another hot day, but I kept feeling shivery. Lots of people passed by: families, couples, oldies with their grandchildren. No guys on their own, though.

I began to count slowly. I'd get to five hundred, I thought, and if no one had come up to me by then, I'd go home. If I wasn't already dead of heart failure.

I'd reached two hundred-and-something when, out of the corner of my eye, I saw someone – I couldn't see whether it was a man or woman, old or young – coming briskly towards me. I knew this was him, *had* to be him, but I was turned to stone, my mouth dry, my breath ragged. I couldn't look, couldn't even glance towards him, could only wait for him to reach me.

When he did, he stopped in front of me. 'Sorry,' he said, smiling. 'This must have been quite an ordeal for you.'

My first thought was one of intense disappointment. He wasn't gorgeous. He wasn't even young. He had short, fair hair cut quite trendily, he had quite a nice face and was, I suppose, good-looking in an old-film-starish way, but he must have been at least forty-five. And I've *never* fancied older men.

He had a wrapped, box-shaped object in his hand and he passed it over. 'Look, this is for you,' he said, and I detected again the faint accent. American?

'No, really,' I said. 'I couldn't.' Not now I'd seen him I couldn't. I didn't know what he was up to, fancying someone years younger than himself, but there was no way I was going to fancy him back.

I swung my rucksack round to the front and rummaged in it, anxious to say my piece and be on my way. 'I just came to give you these things back.'

'Please,' he said, before I could get them out. 'I don't want them. Do keep them.' He tried to give me the wrapped box again. 'And I'd just like you to have this little … '

I shook my head violently, not wanting to encourage him in any way. 'No,' I said. 'No, really. I can't.'

'I just wanted to talk to you.'

He sighed and I stared at the ground, wanting to run, wishing I hadn't come.

'This is really, really difficult, but let me assure you, Holly, I have nothing but good intentions towards you. I don't wish you the slightest harm.'

I didn't say anything. What I thought was, he *would*

say that, wouldn't he? He was hardly going to admit he was a perve.

'Look, I'm not some dodgy old chap trying to get off with a young girl, I can tell you that. My name's Ben Simmons. I was born in England but live in the States and I've got a lovely wife called Jennie at home. She knows all about this, knows about you.'

A threesome! I thought. Pervy or what? How come I got the nutcases?

'I wanted to meet you to say thank you but I'm not interested in your presents or anything.' I blurted out. 'Please don't send any more.'

He gave a small smile. 'Look, I don't blame you for being suspicious. Or for thinking I'm up to no good. It's OK, though, really it is. I'm totally on the level.'

'Then what are you up to?' I looked him in the eye, just swiftly, and noticed something very strange. His right eye was two different colours, like mine. And there was something else. I know you can never really tell, and you see photos of mass murderers where they look completely innocent and like your favourite uncle, but there was something about his face, his expression, which said to me that he was OK. I chewed my lip. 'So why … I mean, if you don't – if it's not that you fancy me or anything dodgy like that, why are you sending me things?'

'Ah,' he said.

I shrugged and waited for an explanation.

'I'm being very selfish in what I'm doing,' he said. 'But then I thought if I didn't tell you … ' He stopped and rubbed his nose and I thought to myself that I'd read somewhere that it was a sign that you weren't telling the truth. And anyway, apart from that, what on earth was he talking about?

'I'd better start at the beginning. Look, d'you want to walk somewhere? Sit down and have a coffee?'

I shook my head. 'No, thanks. I just want to go.'

'OK.' He rubbed his nose again. 'I'll just try and say this as simply as possible. I came into the tea shop a couple of weeks ago. I was looking over old haunts – I've been living in the States for some years now and I'm back here on a three-month contract.'

'Yes?'

'I … well, let's just say I recognised you.'

'*What*? I've never seen you before.'

'Hang on. Let me go on. After I … I recognised you, I worked things out, dates and so on, and talked to some people who know about genetics and stuff, and in the end I just knew that it was true. There were too many coincidences.'

People continued to go by, cars pulled into the car

park. I hoped Mum and Dad wouldn't come back early from Nan and Grandad's and see me standing there with him.

'I don't know what you're talking about,' I said. I began to edge away. Although he looked perfectly normal, it was obvious that the guy was a complete nutter. He was probably going to tell me he was Jesus any minute now.

'I mean, it was a shock to me, but I've had time to get used to it in these last few weeks. And I just couldn't go back to the States without telling you.'

'Telling me what?'

He tried to take my hand. I pulled it away.

'There's no easy way of saying this, Holly, and I know it's going to be a terrible shock to you. You've got the right to know, though.'

I stared at him, speechless, waiting for him to say the thing that would change, ruin and dissolve my life.

'I have to tell you.' He drew in a deep, shuddering breath. 'Holly, you're my daughter.'

chapter seven

I stared at him in horror and disbelief. '*What*? You're mad!' I shouted, and the next thing I remember was pushing him, and then running away through the crowds, tripping over the wheels of a buggy and dropping the little square present which I somehow found I had hold of. I heard a tinkle of broken glass as it landed on the ground but just left it. I steadied myself, apologised to the buggy-owner and ran on.

Behind me, I heard him shout, 'Holly! Come back!'

I don't know whether he started running too, but I knew the area well and the odds were that he didn't. I ran across the forecourt of the palace, dodged down a lane by the river, ran under the bridge and hid behind a large oak tree.

My heart was pounding so loudly I could hear it. Total nightmare! What an absolute nutter!

I gasped, bending over and trying to catch my breath. Mum had been right to decide not to meet him. You just didn't know *what* people were like. And he'd looked nice, too. So reasonable and ordinary. But then, I guessed, so had Jack the Ripper.

So, what was he up to, then? Was he the sort of bloke who preyed on young girls? The type who couldn't hack it with someone his own age, so tried it on with schoolgirls. He'd more than likely have wanted me to dress up in school uniform and call him Daddy. I thought about our uniform at the shop and winced: he'd probably fancied me in that, all cutesy and Victorian doll. He might have taken a photo of me – some of the doodles did. He might have a photo of me in his bedroom at home and … I shuddered.

Should I tell the police? Should I say I was being pestered? But then I shouldn't have agreed to meet him. They'd just say I'd brought it on myself, *asked* for it. I couldn't even tell Mum and Dad.

I leaned against the tree and did deep breathing and very gradually my heart stopped its mad pounding.

I didn't want to go home, and I knew Ella wouldn't

be back yet, so I walked round to Alex's house, running and rerunning the horrible, weird scenario in my head. He'd said *this*, I'd said *that*, and then he'd said …

Alex was in his room playing music so loudly that I could hear it halfway down the road. It took four long rings at his door before he heard me.

He looked ruffled and scruffy, but pleased to see me. 'That's lucky,' he said. 'My mum and dad are out.' He raised his eyebrows meaningfully and I pretended not to know what he meant.

'Something horrible's happened,' I said and I pushed his front door shut behind me and leant on it for a moment, feeling trembly again.

He was on his way into the sitting room and he turned and looked at me. 'What?'

'I went to meet that man.'

'The bloke who's been sending you presents?' he asked, surprised and cross. 'You didn't tell me. What did you want to do that for?'

'I just wanted him to have his stuff back,' I said. 'I was going to give it to him and then go.'

'What was he like, then?'

'Old,' I said.

'How old? Thirty? Sixty? A hundred?'

'About forty,' I said.

We went into the sitting room and sat on the sofa. He put his arm round my shoulders. 'You look really funny,' he said. 'All pale under your freckles.'

'It was horrible.' I pushed my head into Alex's chest as if I could hide there. 'He looked quite ordinary, but – '

'What did he say, then? Something filthy?'

'It wasn't that it was filthy. Not that. Well, it was in a way … ' I broke off.

'You can tell me what he said. I'm not going to be shocked, am I? You'll feel better once you've said it.'

I looked up at him looking all ordinary and safe; a part of my life that I didn't have to worry about. Of course I could tell him.

'He said something *mad*. He said he was my father!' I burst out.

Alex looked at me in astonishment. 'What? And – what? – he wanted you to play games or something?'

I shook my head. 'He just said – ' I put on a slight American accent – ' "Holly, you're my daughter".'

'Blimey,' Alex said. He ran a hand through his hair so that it stuck up even more. 'What a weird thing!' He shook his head. 'What're you going to do?'

'Nothing,' I said. 'Nothing at all. I can't, can I? I

mean, it's not an offence to go round telling people you're their father, is it? I can't even tell my mum about it because I promised her I'd put him off.' As I said this, I thought of something. That previous Sunday when she'd suddenly changed her mind about meeting him, *had she actually seen him standing there?*

Alex opened and closed his mouth, trying to form words. After a moment he said to me quite seriously, 'Look, I'm not being funny, but it's not true, is it?'

'No!' I sat bolt upright, filled with fury and immediately discounting my last thought. 'Of course it's not. How can you even *think* that?'

He shrugged. 'I dunno. It just seems a weird thing for a bloke to come up with. I mean, you hear about some pervy goings-on these days – men who like licking feet and dressing up in nappies and all that – but this doesn't seem the same, really. I mean, why go to all the bother of – '

'I don't know!' I turned on him angrily. 'I've come round here for you to make me feel better, not for you to start questioning me! He's mad! He's a lunatic! How dare he come along and start messing my life up like this?'

'OK, OK, calm down,' Alex said. He patted my head. 'Let's go into the kitchen and I'll make you a coffee. And a sandwich, if you like. My dad cooked some sausages earlier. How about a sausage sandwich?'

'OK,' I muttered.

We had the sausage sandwiches – I was starving – and then we talked a bit more about the madman and what I could do. The answer, of course, was nothing. I had to ignore it. Pretend nothing had happened. I felt a little better when I remembered that he'd said something about being on a three-month contract and going back to the States shortly. But had he been lying about that, too? Could he be completely off his trolley about some things but rational about other things?

We talked about what he'd said again and again, and then we went on to other, more normal things. An hour or so later I was stretched out on the sofa and sort of getting things into perspective when Alex said, 'My mum and dad won't be in until eleven tonight.'

'So?'

'So nothing!' There was a smile twisting up the corners of his mouth. 'It's just that … well, we don't often get a house to ourselves, do we?'

I sat up. 'Are you saying what I think you're saying?'

He shrugged, still with the little smile.

'I don't believe you!'

'What? What have I said?'

'I've had a shock like … like that and you – *you* – want to try it on, don't you? You want me to go upstairs and – '

'Not necessarily upstairs,' he said, trying to be funny.

'Oh, get lost!' I said. I stood up and smoothed down my T-shirt.

'It was just a suggestion,' he said. 'You don't have to get the hump about it.'

'I can't believe you can be so … so *crude*,' I said. 'At a time like this – '

'Look, sorry,' he said. 'I just thought it might help take your mind off things. My mistake.'

'Too right your mistake,' I said. I went into the hall and picked up my rucksack. 'I'm going round to Ella's.'

'Oh, don't,' Alex said, looking at me ruefully, head on one side. 'I said I'm sorry. You know I'd never do anything you didn't want to do.'

I sighed and paused in the hallway. Maybe I was overreacting, but I just didn't feel like doing anything – not even a kiss or a snog, certainly not anything more. And I was really angry with Alex for even thinking that I would. Such an unfeeling, blokeish thing to do.

'All right, I forgive you,' I said. 'But I'm still going round to Ella's. I just want to see what she says.'

'Ah, the lovely little Holly!' the pillock said, answering the door to me. 'I do hope we're not prickly today.'

I managed to drag a smile out. It was difficult because he was wearing a yellow sweatshirt with something disgusting down the front and it was all I could do not to shudder and rush past him. 'Is Ella in, please?' I asked.

'Judging by the *noise* … ' He rolled his eyes and pointed upwards. 'I think she must be.'

I went past him and up to Ella's room. I could feel him looking at me all the way up the stairs.

Within ten minutes, I'd told Ella the whole scenario. Her reaction was the same as Alex's.

'That's just crazy,' she said, and then she looked at me, bewildered. 'But what's he get out of that, then?'

I shrugged. 'Dunno. Maybe he goes round the country pretending he has daughters everywhere. Like a sailor has a girl in every port, you know?'

'That's seriously weird.'

'You're telling me.'

She was silent for a moment, and then she said. 'I wonder what the thing was in the box?'

I shook my head.

'I wonder if he'll send anything else now, or just leave it?'

I shook my head again. I just didn't know.

Ella and I decided not to go to the cinema after all, so I was home when Mum and Dad returned from Nan's. Dad went into the kitchen and started making one of his fresh tomato pizzas, leaving me in the sitting room with Mum, watching TV while she ironed a couple of uniforms for work – she's a booking-in clerk at a hospital and she had an early shift the next day.

I'd found out from Ella what stalls there had been at the craft fair and told Mum about them. 'There wasn't anything really interesting,' I said. 'Loads of picture frames. More stalls selling those than anything else.'

'Did you buy any earrings?'

'Nope. Couldn't see any I liked.' I looked at her hopefully. 'Do you want your fiver back?'

'Course I don't. I dare say you'll find some in the week that you want to buy.' She finished the uniforms, put the iron to one side and folded up the board. 'Did you ... you haven't heard anything else all week, then?'

I knew immediately what she meant and felt my cheeks beginning to go red. 'Nope. Nothing at all.'

'You would tell me, wouldn't you, Holly?'

'Course I would.'

'I know you think I'm terribly nosy, but I'm just concerned for your welfare. It comes with being a mum, see. We just can't help it.'

'Yeah, I know.' My mind suddenly churned with questions. OK, the man was a lunatic; I had complete faith in my mum and dad being who I'd always thought they were, and the whole idea was ridiculous – but ... if I could just ask a few things to be perfectly, utterly sure.

How could I ask *anything*, though, without admitting to myself that there was just the tiniest grain of doubt?

'I don't suppose he was the Leonardo di Caprio love of my life, anyway,' I said. 'He was probably just some old geezer ... ' I gave a short laugh. 'I don't expect the love of my life will come along for years and years.'

'So it's not Alex? The love of your life, I mean,' Mum asked.

'Nah! Doubt it.' I pretended to consider things. 'I mean, how often do you meet the right guy when you're sixteen?'

'Not very often, I shouldn't think,' Mum said. 'Most people change a great deal between sixteen and twenty-five. At the end of those years you sometimes end up being a completely different person.'

I nodded, as if considering this. 'So when you met Dad, did you think straight away that he was – ' I lowered my voice dramatically – '*the one*?'

'No, I certainly didn't,' Mum said, laughing.

'Did you have a lot of other boyfriends?'

'One or two,' Mum said.

'Serious ones?' I asked suddenly. 'Did you wish you'd married someone else?'

Mum looked up at me sharply. 'Of course not!' she said. 'Dad and I are a very happy couple. What on earth made you ask that?'

I swallowed hard. 'Oh, nothing.' I said airily. 'Just interested.'

Just – suddenly – very interested.

chapter eight

'They've rung!' Ella said the following Wednesday.
'What? Who have?'

It was a quarter to nine and we were in the staffroom getting into our gear, adjusting our hats on our heads so they looked less awful and fluffing out our skirts.

'Them. The helpline about my dad!'

'Really? What did they say?'

Stacey and Mandy weren't listening, they were too busy anguishing over their hats, but Ella lowered her voice anyway. 'They said they may have a lead.'

'Really?'

'Someone saw his name on Teletext and rang in to say someone of that name is working in their local garage.'

'Really? What local garage? Round here, d'you mean?'

Ella shook her head. 'They wouldn't say. They don't tell you that; it could be anywhere in the country.'

'What happens now, then?'

'They write to him at this garage to see if he really is my dad and they ask him if he's got the same birth date and everything. If it's not him, they say he'll probably write back and tell them. If it *is* him, they send the letter from me – the one we wrote.'

'And then?'

'Then just see what happens,' Ella said. She gave a shiver. 'Maureen said not to build my hopes up too much, it was just a lead. It might not be my dad after all.'

I smiled at her in what was meant to be a bracing sort of way. 'It might, though.'

'OK, girls!' Upstairs, Mrs Potter was about to turn over the 'Open for fresh cream cakes' sign on the front door.

'What about you? He hasn't been in touch, has he?' Ella said as we went up the stairs.

I shook my head. 'I think I might have mentioned it if he had!'

'No more presents, either. That's a bit of a shame.

It's not every day you get someone splashing money on you, is it?'

'I don't want loony money, thank you very much,' I said.

When I got home from work that night, I went up to my room and stared at my reflection in the mirror. I was looking at *that eye*. That eye that was the same as the man's eye.

Why hadn't I told Ella or Alex about that identical two-coloured eye, one part brown, one part blue?

The answer was: because I'd been worried that they'd pick up on it. Say, 'That's odd,' or 'That's a bit of a coincidence, isn't it?' or 'Maybe there's something in it after all.'

But there couldn't be *something* in it, could there? It couldn't be *partly* true. Either it was, or it wasn't. Either I was, or I wasn't.

No, I couldn't possibly be. How could I? But then why had Mum suddenly changed her mind like that?

I flopped down on my bed. I had to think.

We'd done a mock trial in our drama class last year: the trial of Richard III. The object was to decide whether he'd killed the princes in the Tower or not.

I'd been chosen as part of his defence team, and

when we'd started, like everyone else in class, I'd thought he was guilty. My reasoning went like this: we'd already done the Shakespeare play of the same name, and everyone knew old Shakespeare was a genius, so it wasn't likely he'd got it wrong, was it? Richard III was a killer and that was that.

Jim O'Toole, our drama teacher, had told us that Shakespeare wasn't necessarily writing the truth, though. He'd said Shakespeare was writing for the stage, to make the best dramatic impact – and also to suit the king who was on the throne at the time. O'Toole said we were to look at the facts.

So when I investigated properly (reference library, historical documents, the whole bit) I found that the facts – the true historical facts – didn't match the play. I then wrote everything up and constructed what I thought was a brilliant defence for old Richard III so that by the end of the month, after the mock trial and witnesses and everything, everyone in the class – including the prosecution – thought he was innocent.

And that was what I had to do now. Look at the facts, coldly and dispassionately. Look at the facts as if my whole world wasn't going to crumble if the result wasn't what I wanted it to be, if the dad I'd known and loved all my life wasn't … But no, he *had* to be!

I'd been born on Christmas Eve 1984. So that meant Mum had got pregnant with me in March 1984. She and Dad had got married in July 1980, so the first thing I had to find out was whether they were getting on all right in 1984. Had Dad worked away from home at that time? Had they had a terrible row? Had they had a trial separation or something? It was possible. They wouldn't have later told me, would they?

I started to think along those lines and then I pulled myself up short. *What was I doing?* I was allowing the madman to influence me! I was actually questioning, if only in my head, my mum and dad's marriage and the identity of my father. I was jeopardising my family because of him. No! He wouldn't drive me mad. I wouldn't let him!

I jumped up, went downstairs and put the TV on. I put it on quietly, because Mum, being on early shift, was in her room having a nap.

Because I was on my own, though, pretty soon I started to think more things. About descriptions and appearances, for instance.

Mum's quite tall for a woman, one metre sixty-eight, whereas Dad is quite short for a man, about one metre seventy. I'm nearly as tall as him. This man, the madman, had seemed very tall. Over one metre eighty, I thought.

Dad has mousy dark hair and hazel eyes. Mum has got very dark hair and brown eyes. I have blond hair and one blue and one odd eye. The madman has very blond hair and one blue and one odd eye.

What else? Dad's a bit older than Mum, he's fifty-six, and Mum's fifty. The madman seemed to be about forty-five, so he was younger than Mum. Dad was forty when they had me, Mum was thirty-four and he, say, was about twenty-nine. I didn't know what this proved.

The only other thing, which shouldn't have come into the equation but did, somehow, was that Dad wasn't all that attractive. He was gorgeous and cuddly, of course, but he had a paunch and was balding and wore old-fashioned clothes and glasses. If you gave him an attractiveness rating from 1 to 10 he'd get about 3, whereas Mum, despite her age, would get about 8. The madman, much as I hated to admit it, would be about an 8 too. I only thought about this because I'd read in a magazine just a few days before that you were usually attracted to people who had about the same attractiveness rating as yourself.

Unbidden, a picture of Mum and the madman

came into my head. Somehow, horribly, they matched; seemed to go together as a couple. Both tall, good-looking, quite striking in their own way.

They went together, actually, better than Mum and Dad did.

I pulled myself up again. How could I even *think* that? I switched between channels hurriedly, looking for something to interest me.

We usually have a takeaway curry once a week, and Dad came in with this about six thirty. Mum had finished her nap by then and was up, warming the plates, chopping up cucumber and mixing it with yogurt to make raita.

While we ate, I looked at Dad searchingly for evidence, for traits that I'd inherited from him. I looked for things to prove that he was my dad. *My dad.* I couldn't possibly believe that he wasn't. It would be like suddenly finding out that the world was flat or the sky was falling in.

What I discovered was (a) his nose. His nostrils were wide at the bottom and so were mine. (b) His hair (what he had left) grew from a little peak at the front, so did mine. This bit of evidence was a bit woolly, though, because Mum's hair grew like that as well. Widow's peak, she called it. So that left (c) Dad loved really hot curry, so did I. Mum hated it, that was why she always made raita to cool it down.

Not much to tie me to Dad, then – but apart from Mum and me both being tall and having quite slanty eyes, I didn't think I was much like *her*, either.

Maybe I didn't belong to either of them. Maybe I was adopted, then.

I thought of this with a forkful of chicken masala halfway to my mouth. No, I'd never believe *that*. Mum and I got on so well. We shared jokes and giggled at people we saw in the street and only had to look at each other to know what the other was thinking.

But then Ella and I were like that, too, so perhaps that was something that just grew.

'What's up, love? Chew on a cardamom?' Dad asked.

I started eating again. It did no good thinking about things, no good at all. I had to either believe in my mum and dad or not. Put up or shut up.

I thought I meant that, but even while I was still thinking it, another part of me was planning where I could go next, how I could find out what had gone on earlier in their marriage.

'God, it's awful round Ella's house!' I suddenly heard myself saying. 'Every time I see Ella she tells me about some big argument or other.'

Mum tutted. 'I don't know how people can live like that. It's the kids I feel sorry for. What age are Ella's brothers?'

'Nine and thirteen – and they hate the pillock, too,' I said. 'They do nothing but argue with him. Ella thinks this house is like a peace camp by comparison.' I reached for a poppadom, then asked casually, 'Haven't you ever rowed, you two?'

Mum laughed. 'Dad isn't the rowing type,' she said.

'So you've always got on, have you?' What I longed to ask was: *You didn't have a huge break-up about 1984?*

Mum gave me a funny look. I couldn't work out what it meant.

'No marriage is a bed of roses,' Dad said after a moment.

'Ooh, cliché, cliché!' I said.

'Well, you know what I mean. Every relationship has to be worked at,' Dad said. 'The more you put into one, the more you'll get out.'

That was quite profound, coming from him. A dad of few words, is my dad.

Yes, he *had* to be my dad.

90

And yet, and yet …

I hardly slept that night, just kept rolling around twisting my sheets up, thinking things, wondering and worrying about it.

But the next day I knew what I had to do. I phoned the madman's mobile number from work and left another message. I was really angry; I said I didn't believe a word of it and it was all a mistake, but I wanted to know why he'd done it. I said I'd be at the same meeting place on Friday evening at six o'clock, so that he could explain.

chapter nine

My anger lasted right up until Friday after work. Which was lucky, because if I'd really thought about what I was doing, I might not have had the nerve to do it. I just felt furious, though. Why had he done it? I couldn't believe the nerve of the bloke. What did he hope to get out of it? Why pick on me?

I would tell him what I thought of him and say I'd report him to the police if he told lies about my family or ever harassed me again. It was worse than stalking, I'd say, and there were laws against men like him.

He was twenty minutes late arriving. When the palace clock struck a quarter past the hour I felt relieved and triumphant. Ha! Couldn't go through with it, eh? Couldn't face me. I stood there thinking smugly that I'd give him until six thirty and then go home, and after that I'd never give him another thought as long as I lived.

He arrived at six twenty, though, rushing across from the direction of the station, dressed in a suit and carrying a navy canvas briefcase thing.

As soon as I saw him, I lost my nerve and began to feel sick. Why couldn't he have chickened out? Why did I have to go through all this? He was a complete pig to make me suffer.

I stared at him bleakly without saying anything. He was taller than I remembered, his haircut was very American, and he had fair skin with faint freckles across his forehead.

'Sorry,' he said. 'The traffic was horrendous. Must have increased sixfold since I lived here.'

I looked at him and just wanted to run. Now. Quickly. Before he could speak.

'I know this is an ordeal for you, Holly,' he said. 'I feel the biggest bastard in the world for putting you through it.'

Before he could say another word. If I went now, I wouldn't hear anything I didn't want to hear …

'Look. Let's just go and have a coffee somewhere, shall we? I won't say anything about – about you

know what. I just want to talk to you. Just maybe …
get to know you a bit. That's all.'

He put out an arm to propel me along but I shied
away, not wanting to be touched by him. 'There's a
buffet thing open at the station,' I said.

'Fine. Or would you rather go somewhere else?' he
asked. 'Out of town a bit?'

I shook my head mutely. I wasn't going to go anywhere with a madman. The buffet would have to do.

'It's OK there,' I muttered.

In silence we walked to the station, and in silence
we went into the buffet and I sat down. While he
went up to the counter, I looked round. There didn't
seem to be anyone I knew – just a few lingering
tourists and people who worked at the palace waiting
for the next train back into London.

He brought back two coffees and put them down
on the table. He stared at me hard for a while, until,
embarrassed, I muttered, 'For Christ's sake!' under my
breath. Then he said, 'Sorry,' and hid his face in his
hands.

This was just as bad. Worse. I didn't know what
to do or say. I was terrified he'd start crying or
something.

'Do you come from round here?' I asked quickly.

Polite, superficial conversation, but it was all I could think of.

'Used to,' he said. He lowered his hands from his face 'Way back.'

'Where d'you live now?'

'Monterey,' he said. 'California. D'you know it?'

I shook my head.

'It's on the Pacific coast and it's beautiful. It's an old trading bay – it used to belong to the Mexicans and there are lots of their houses around. Have you heard of *Cannery Row*?'

'The book?' I asked.

He nodded.

'Yeah. We did Steinbeck in school last year.'

'*Cannery Row* is in Monterey. It's a bit touristy now, but it's still pretty amazing.'

'And you live right there?'

He nodded. 'My wife and I have got a beautiful Victorian house right on the front facing the ocean. We can sit in the front garden and watch the dolphins and sea lions messing about on the rocks.'

I looked outside the buffet, at the station with its green, peeling paint and dead flower baskets. 'You must hate it when you have to come here, then.'

'This is my first trip back for seventeen years,' he

said. 'I'm an American citizen now.' He lifted the coffee cup to his lips and I didn't look at him, but I could see that his hand was trembling.

'Why have you done this?' I suddenly blurted out. 'Why did you want to come here and try to mess up my life?'

He put the coffee cup down and paused, as if collecting his thoughts. 'I'm over here for three months, right?' he began. 'Years ago – when I was a kid – I used to live about ten miles away, but I'd never done the tourist bit, been to the palace or anything. As weekends tend to be pretty lonely, I decided to get out and hit the tourist trail, the tourist bit was just my sort of thing. And then when I was here I thought I'd go in and have a sandwich at the tea shop. Ye Olde Tea Shoppe,' he said, pronouncing the 'e' on the end of the words and smiling slightly.

I didn't respond, just sat staring out of the window.

'I saw you. You ... you look very much like your mom did, so I kind of recognised you immediately. It's not so much looks and colouring – because your mom's dark, isn't she, and you're fair – but you've got the same thick, straight hair and slanted cat's eyes. You twist a strand of hair round and round your finger just the way she does, too, and you've got two big

96

front teeth.' He smiled to himself as if he was remembering a joke. Don't you remember me staring at you?'

I shook my head. 'We're usually pretty rushed in there. I don't remember you at all.'

'I came in again, just to make sure. You didn't serve me – I think you were looking after a kid's birthday party.'

There was a pause and I knew he was waiting for me to ask what it was he'd wanted to make sure about, but I didn't.

'When I came in the first time,' he said, 'after I'd got over the shock of recognising your mom in you, I noticed your eye. Same as mine, right?'

'So?' I said.

'And then your colouring. You're not like your mom, are you?'

'So?' I said again, more aggressively.

'I thought that you … you had my colouring. And then I thought about your name. You were born at Christmas, weren't you, with a name like that? Well, I told you I used to live here, but then in March 1984 I went off to live in the States. Before I went, me and Allie – your mom – had a weekend away – '

'No!' My eyes suddenly filled with tears. 'Don't say things like that! I'll go if you start!'

He stopped speaking immediately and passed me a handkerchief out of his suit pocket. 'I'm sorry,' he said. 'I'm really sorry. This is a real bum thing to do to you.'

I buried my face in the hanky, which smelled of soap and aftershave.

'All along the way I've been ringing my wife Jennie about it, asking for advice. She said it would eat me up if I didn't say anything to you. She didn't tell me how to go about it, though. There's no etiquette for this kind of thing, is there?'

I didn't reply. I felt like I might be dreaming.

'You see,' he went on gently, 'we have a great life and we've got everything a couple could want – except kids. Jennie can't have any children. We thought about adoption and everything but time went on and I'm forty-six now and there are so many rules and regulations that the whole thing got just impossible.'

Outside the window, life went on as usual. Inside, my life was slowly cracking up. But only if I believed him.

'We thought about a Third World adoption and we even started negotiating through an agency in China to get a baby, but that came to nothing. We got older and we'd more or less resigned ourselves to not having kids. And then I came here and saw you and suddenly everything changed. My life was turned on its head. I'd found the one thing that had been missing from it. Can you imagine how I felt?'

I could. *But only if I believed him.*

I stood up. 'Sorry,' I said. 'I'm just not taking this. I don't believe you. It's all a pack of lies. I don't know why you've done it but I don't intend to play along. I'm not going to be part of it.'

'Holly, I – '

'Don't talk to me. Don't ever get in touch again. I hate you! Even if you *were* my father, I'd hate you!'

'I know you're terribly upset and – '

I didn't wait to hear any more, just ran out of the door, across the station and towards home. When I got halfway there I found I was clutching his handkerchief, and I just let it drop into the gutter.

'Blimey!' Alex said when I'd finished telling him. 'A right nutter, eh?'

'Absolutely barking,' I said. 'People like that should be locked up.'

I'd run nearly all the way home, but when I'd come in sight of my house I'd realised I couldn't face seeing them. I'd gone round to Alex's house and we'd come out for a walk by the river.

'But … I mean, how weird is it that he knows your mum's name and everything?' He looked at me sideways. 'And it's bit of a coincidence about your eye and all.'

'That's all it is – a coincidence,' I said. 'There must be millions of people with eyes like mine!'

I said that – but I'd never met anyone. I stopped by the steps where the pleasure boats pulled in during the day, and stared at the river. I didn't have to believe it. I could just pull a curtain over the whole thing. He – the nutter – would be going back to America soon so he'd be out of the way. I could forget he'd ever spoken to me.

But I wasn't the sort of person who could do that. I knew I had to find out the truth. *Had to*: if I didn't I would be lying to myself. It would be like knowing that the evidence existed to save Richard III, but pretending it didn't.

I sat down on the stone steps and Alex sat down next to me, slinging a casual arm round my shoulders. Since the last time, he knew better than to come on heavy.

'Have you thought … I mean, what about asking

your mum? You get on well with her, don't you? Couldn't you just drop some hints?'

'How can I? What would I say? Oh, by the way, Mum, some bloke's told me he's my real dad. Did you have an illicit affair and betray my dad seventeen years ago and forget about it?'

Alex snorted. 'Maybe not quite like that. What about asking one of your mum's friends? Or hasn't she got a sister or someone?

'She's an only child,' I said. 'Like me. And she hasn't got any really close women friends. Not ones that I think she'd tell something like that to.'

'You can have a test, can't you? To prove if he's the father. I heard about a guy at college who had one when his girlfriend tried to prove he was the father of her baby.'

I sighed. 'It all sounds a bit drastic. I … I'll look round and see what I can find around the house. I'll ask them things, make enquiries. But if I find out it's true I'm going to run away!' I burst out. 'I'll never want to see my mum again.'

Alex squeezed my shoulder. 'I don't suppose it'll come to that,' he said. 'It'll be all right. It's too – too radical to be true.'

'Course it is,' I said, and I sighed again.

chapter ten

The next morning I stayed in bed until ten thirty, until Mum called up that there was a bacon sandwich waiting and did I fancy going shopping with her because she wanted to go to the craft centre.

I put on my dressing gown and went down. Dad was outside fiddling with the car and Mum was having a coffee and, I noticed, a cigarette – which she'd given up about five years ago.

'You've started smoking again,' I said. 'Why's that?'

'Oh, I haven't really started,' she said. 'I'm only having five a day. I know it's a disgusting habit but – well, sometimes you just feel in need of a little something extra, don't you?'

'Do you?' I said. 'You wouldn't like it if I said that.'

I looked at the ashtray. 'Only five a day? You've already had three of them this morning.'

She shrugged, stubbed out the one she was smoking and swept the contents of the ashtray into the bin. 'I'll stop again soon,' she said. 'I know your dad hates it.'

I looked at her sharply when she said that, as if she might have given herself away on the words *your dad*; as if a jagged fork of lightning might have come from heaven and struck her dead.

She didn't even blush, though. I ate my bacon sandwich in silence, thinking deeply.

'Coming to the craft place, then?' Mum said. 'We can have a bit of lunch there.'

The craft store was in an out-of-town shopping centre and they also had shops selling pictures and mirrors and candles and stuff. We nearly always bought something for my bedroom when we were there and had a nice lunch out, usually something prawny.

'I don't think I will,' I said.

Mum looked at me in surprise. 'Oh. Have you arranged to see Ella, then? She can come with us if she likes.'

I shook my head. 'I just don't fancy going.'

She looked at me again, more searchingly. I didn't look up, but pretended to be pulling a bit of fat off my bacon.

'Ella hasn't heard anything,' I said.

'What – about her dad?'

I nodded.

'I'm not surprised.' Mum began stacking the dishwasher. 'When families break up, people tend to make new lives for themselves. It's sad, but there it is.'

'You'd think someone's *dad*, though, would keep in touch. I mean, if you and Dad split up, he'd want to keep in touch with me, wouldn't he?'

'Of course he would. That's different, though. You're practically grown-up. You'd keep in touch with him yourself.'

'You wouldn't ever split up, though, would you?'

'Of course not!' She turned round from the dishwasher in surprise. 'Is that why you've been a bit funny lately? You've seen Ella's mum with that new man and you're worried about me and Dad?'

I shrugged.

'Darling!' Mum hitched up her skirt so it was a mini, and stuck her bust out. 'I'm not like Ella's mum, am I?'

I gave a sickly grin.

'Dad and I are absolutely fine! We're like Darby and Joan now.'

'Who are Darby and Joan?'

Mum pulled a bemused face. 'I'm not exactly sure. You say that when you're talking about a couple who've been together for years and years and have sort of moulded into each other.'

I nodded slowly. It wasn't *now* I was interested in, though. It was *then*. In 1984.

'You would tell me, wouldn't you?' I asked suddenly. 'You wouldn't just let me find out for myself?'

'If Dad and I were heading for the rocks?' she laughed. 'Of course I'd tell you.'

But I hadn't meant that, of course. I'd meant, would she tell me if I was someone else's daughter, and not Dad's?

I didn't go to the craft centre. Dad went off to play a round of golf and I said I was going to stay in and catch up with some reading for next term. I wasn't going to read, though, what I was going to do was have a nose round the house.

I knew where my birth certificate was: in the middle drawer of the bureau in the sitting room. I'd had it out a couple of years before when I'd applied for a passport. I had a look at it again, though, just to make sure there was nothing I'd missed. It said:

Mother's name: Alice Stephanie Devine, nee Ritchie
Father's name: Gordon James Devine

I stared at it as if it could give up some secret. As if the words *not really* might suddenly appear under the 'Father's name' bit.

I looked at everything else in the drawer. There were Mum's and Dad's birth certificates, their marriage certificate and a death certificate for my other gran – Mum's mum – who'd died the previous year. There was a baby weight chart of mine showing my progress from 7lb 1oz upwards and also a pink wristband saying Baby Devine which they'd put on in the hospital when I'd been born. In a transparent envelope were all my baby congratulation cards. I'd looked through them before, of course; I'd loved looking through them when I was little because they said things like 'To your beautiful baby girl' and 'Your baby girl comes with all the love in the world' and gooey stuff like that. This time I searched through them just in case there was one from someone called Ben.

Of course there wasn't. I looked through the rest of the stuff in the other drawers of the bureau, and then I looked all along the bookshelves and between the books as well. I didn't know what I was looking for – as if I was going to find a letter from him, the mad-man, stuck between Ruth Rendell and Joanna Trollope. I did find something a bit funny, though: there was a book called *The Poetry of Love* and when I got it down and looked in the front for clues to see if it said 'to someone' or 'from someone', I saw that the first page had been torn out. I then found another poetry book where the same thing had happened. This led me to think that someone – it had to be Mum – had received the books as a present from a man she shouldn't have done, so she'd torn out the front page where the man had written an inscription.

In the middle of all this research the phone rang and it was Ella.

'You didn't ring me!' she said accusingly. 'You didn't ring to let me know how you got on last night.'

'Sorry.' I told her what had happened, more or less, and she said all the right things about him being a weirdo and a perve. When I'd finished, though, there was a long pause and she said, 'God, it's weird about you having the same eye as him, though, isn't it?'

I sighed. 'Yeah, I know,' I said. 'Look, I'll meet you later. Mum and Dad are both out so I'm just doing a few investigations here first.'

'Oh, get you, Sherlock,' she said. 'Good luck.'

I started looking upstairs, in Mum and Dad's bedroom. I felt uneasy doing this because I didn't want to find anything dodgy. Not about *him*, dodgy, but any condoms or rude books or anything. Earlier in the year Ella had found a basque in her mum's room. Just on the chair, not even hidden. I hadn't known what a basque was, and Ella had explained that it was a form of tarty underwear, red nylon with black trimmings, with a laced-up midriff that was supposed to push your boobs up and suspenders so you could wear stockings with it. We imagined her mum putting it on and prancing round in front of the pillock and screamed with horror at the thought.

There was nothing like that here, though, the room was all very stylish: pale-yellow walls washed over with white so that they looked patchy and tastefully faded, and a white cotton duvet cover piled with broderie anglaise cushions. There was an old pine table in the corner of their room and Mum had piles of coloured boxes on this, each containing various bits and pieces: craft stuff, cuttings from magazines, colour charts for the rooms, old bills, letters from relatives and friends, a few photos – stuff like that.

I opened a couple of boxes and leafed through, but

it all looked quite boringly normal. In the middle of the big purple file labelled *Household Bits*, though, was a brown envelope, stuck down, with *Stuff about water meter* written on it in Mum's writing.

This looked funny to me. Why put something like that in a brown envelope and seal it down?

Carefully, I lifted the flap. It wasn't very well stuck – it looked as if she'd opened it herself a couple of times and glued it down again.

Inside were five things. Or six if you count the water-meter folder they were hidden in.

Horrified, legs wobbly, I sat down on the bed and looked through them. First there was a photo of *him*, much younger. He had very blond hair and quite a lot of freckles, and was wearing a black polo neck jumper. There were also the two front pages from the poetry books downstairs, one saying, 'Page 18 sums it all up, darling' and the other, 'Love for always, Ben'. Lastly there were two letters addressed to the house on the other side of town we'd moved from ten years ago. They were postmarked Monterey, one had a date of 1984 and the other 1985.

I didn't actually read them; I reckoned I'd seen enough without sinking quite *that* low. I looked at everything carefully once more, just to make quite sure I'd got things right and wasn't hallucinating, and then I put each thing back carefully inside the water-meter folder and inside the envelope just the way I'd found them.

I sat down on the bed, shaking all over. I sat there for half an hour or so, absolutely immobile, just staring at a piece of fluff on the carpet. I felt I could stay there for ever, quite frozen, and that if I could do that it would be the best thing, because I wouldn't have to take my place in the world again.

The phone rang, though, and brought me back to life. I didn't answer it, but still trance-like, got my bag and a jumper ready to go round to Ella's house. Going downstairs, I got the two poetry books off the bookshelf and put them on the table in the sitting room for a clue. I wanted Mum to know that I knew.

As I was doing this, though, I heard her key in the lock. My first thought was to run out of the back, but before I could do so the door opened and she breezed straight into the sitting room with her bag over her shoulder and two carriers.

'It was *so* crowded!' she said. 'And I couldn't decide on anything. I needed you there to make up my mind for me.' She looked at me curiously. 'You've got a funny look on your face. What've you been doing?'

I swallowed hard. 'Not much,' I said, and my voice sounded all strange and false. 'Reading poetry.'

She looked puzzled. 'What for?'

I tapped the two books on the table meaningfully. 'From *these* poetry books here.'

'What, for next term, d'you mean?'

She still didn't get it.

'These two books. Are they yours?'

She frowned and came over to look at them. 'Mine? Yes, I suppose so. I haven't looked at them for years. Why d'you ask?'

My heart thudded. 'Did you have an affair in 1984?'

'*What*?' She looked insulted and confused. 'What're you talking about?'

'An affair. You had one, didn't you? With some bloke called Ben. He bought you these books.'

'What utter rubbish!' she said, but she went bright red and I didn't think I'd ever seen her go red before. 'That's absolutely outrageous! Whatever's made you say that? Who have you been talking to?'

'I don't need to talk to anyone,' I said. 'I've found the evidence.'

'What evidence? What're you talking about?'

'I've been upstairs looking for stuff … '

She stared at me in horror. 'How dare you! How could you? I've always respected your secrets completely. I wouldn't dream of prying into *your* private things.'

'Yeah, well, very sorry,' I said. I spoke all cockily but I was shaking inside. 'Things like this are important, though. I had to find out, didn't I?'

She let the bags drop on to the floor. She was breathing hard and fast, as if she'd been running. 'What … what have you found out?'

'You had an affair with some bloke called Ben Simmons.'

She moved towards the nearest chair and sat on it. 'Dad's not in at the moment, is he?'

I shook my head.

She ran a hand through her hair. 'I don't know what's got into you. How could you possibly think such a thing? How … how could you think it of me?'

'Quite easily,' I said.

She opened her mouth to speak several times while I just stared at her dispassionately, biding my time before I moved on to the next bombshell.

She pulled at a strand of hair nervously. 'Who's been saying these things?'

'Him, for a start.'

'But how … ?' She turned quickly to face me. 'Have you met him, then?'

I nodded. 'I have now,' I said. 'And now I know why you went so weird when we went to meet him. Why you drove off in such a hurry. You saw him standing there, didn't you?'

She didn't seem to be listening. 'But why should he … after all this time? Why stir up old … ? I mean … '

'You did have an affair with him, then?' I asked bluntly. 'You betrayed Dad and had an affair.'

She started chewing at her inside lip. 'Look, Holly, there's a lot you don't understand. About marriage and so on.'

'Did you or didn't you?'

'It was a … just a fling. There was no way it was ever going to be more than that, and no way I ever wanted anyone to find out. It was over years ago.

'How could you do that to Dad?' I burst out.

She sighed. 'You don't understand. Dad and I weren't getting on very well. He was working long hours and we just didn't seem to have anything to say to each other.'

'That's no excuse.'

'You don't understand,' she said again.

'Too right I don't!'

'When you're older and know a bit more about the world, you'll be better able to deal with things like this. It's a sad fact of life, but I'm afraid people do have affairs sometimes.'

'Does Dad know?' I asked bluntly.

'No. He doesn't. And there's no need for him to know, either. Why should he be hurt?'

I drew in a breath and it felt harsh and raw in my throat. 'He should know, though, shouldn't he? He's been looking after me all these years. He's got every right to know.'

'What d'you mean?' she said, alarmed. 'What're you talking about?'

'Dad's not my dad, is he? He's not my *real* dad.'

'Of course he is!'

'That bloke is. That Ben Simmons. Some stupid American!'

'He is not!'

But I was getting into my stride now and wouldn't be stopped. 'You were married to my dad but you had sex with some bloke and got pregnant and thought you'd got away with it, didn't you? You thought no one would find out your secret. What, did *he* go away and then you had some big reconciliation with Dad and – surprise surprise! – found you were pregnant?'

Mum was crying now, and so was I.

'It wasn't like … I promise you … your dad is who you've always thought he was!'

'I don't believe you! You've lied for years and years and you're lying now!' She got up and tried to put her arms round me but I pushed her away. 'You're just like Ella's mum! You're just a slapper. A slag!'

'Holly! Don't. Please don't – '

'How many other men did you sleep with?' I sobbed. 'Are you sleeping with anyone now?'

'Of course not. Don't … darling … you're just upsetting yourself.'

'What's Dad going to say? Are you going to tell him I'm not his daughter? I'm a bit of a mongrel, aren't I? Mixed parentage. I bet you panicked when you found out you were having me. I bet you tried to get rid of me!'

I pushed the words out between sobs. 'And that's why you wouldn't let me meet him that Sunday. You knew it was him. You saw him standing there!'

'He is *not* your father, Holly! And neither he nor anyone else dare say that he is!'

'He is my father! He wants me to take a test to prove it!' I was lying, of course, but that hardly mattered right then. 'And I'm going to! I'm going to prove that you're a lying cow!'

'Why are you doing this?' Mum stood in front of me, crying and holding out her arms. 'You're my daughter and I love you.'

'It's a bit late for all that,' I said bitterly. 'You should have told me the truth. And you should have told Dad.' I looked her full in the face and spoke coldly. 'You're a wicked liar as well as a slag!'

'Don't call me that!'

'I'm going out now.'

'Where?'

'Does it matter? You care so little about me you won't even tell me who my father is. How can it matter where I'm going?'

'Holly!'

I picked up my things and made for the door.

'Let's talk about it!' she said, making a grab for me. 'We need to talk, Holly. Don't just go off like this!'

'It's a bit late for talking,' I said. 'Sixteen bloody years too late!'

chapter eleven

I cried all the way round to Ella's house, twenty minutes of solid crying, so by the time I got there I was a soggy mess.

The pillock opened the door. I hung my head so that he couldn't see my face properly and asked if Ella was in.

'Well, if it isn't young Holly!' he said. 'And how is young Holly today? Not too cheerful, by the look of it.'

I sniffed long and hard and looked up at him. He was wearing blue nylon tracksuit bottoms and a check jumper, too short. His back-to-front hair was combed over his bald spot and looked as if it was stuck down. 'Is Ella in, please?' I said again.

'I do believe she is. If that row from her bedroom is

anything to go by.' He opened the door wider. 'Come in, come in! I can see you're all set for a girlie afternoon. Problems with your love life, is it?'

I slipped through the door, trying not to let any part of me brush against him.

'Yeah, something like that,' I said.

'Up you go then, Holly Golightly,' he smirked.

Ella hadn't heard any of this because of the music blasting out. Since the last time I'd been, her bedroom had turned into a jumble sale and her bed into bunk beds ready to share it on some weekends with the pillock's nine-year-old daughter. Some of the daughter's possessions (teddy, clothes, Barbie, books) were on the top bunk, and there were other things which I knew weren't Ella's (lava lamp, games, fluffy toy kitten) on the the floor.

Ella was lying on her bed. She jumped up when she saw me and stepped through the mess to turn down the volume on her CD player. 'What's up?' She looked at me, gasped, pulled a wodge of tissues out of a box and handed them over. 'Did you find out something awful?'

I nodded. 'It's all true. My mum did have an affair with him. She's a slag,' I said bitterly. 'I found these letters and stuff ... ' I told Ella about the things I'd found in the box file. 'And then just as I was coming round here she came home and I had it all out with her.'

'You didn't!' Ella's mouth dropped into an amazed gape. 'Oh, gawd! What did she say?'

I slumped on to the bed. I felt exhausted and fed up with crying. 'Nothing much. She more or less admitted it. Said she'd had a fling with him.'

'So he ... that bloke *is* your dad? She said he was?'

I shook my head. 'She wouldn't admit that. She said she'd had the affair but swore that he wasn't my dad.'

'D'you think that's true?'

I shook my head again. 'Course not. All the dates match. And he's got my colouring, and what about my eye and everything? There's just too much,' I added miserably.

For ages, Ella didn't say anything, just sat down beside me and patted me on the shoulder. Then she said, 'It's not fair, is it?'

'What isn't?'

'You've got two dads and I haven't got any.'

I managed a weak smile. 'What's worse,' I said, 'two dads or none at all?'

'None at all,' she said straight away.

I shrugged. 'I'm not going to fall out with you about it.'

I couldn't think about Ella right then. After all, she'd had loads of time to get used to things – she'd grown up with a succession of uncles in the house so had had years and years of knowing her mum was a tart, whereas I'd only just found out about mine.

Ella put some music on and we stayed upstairs until about seven o'clock, and by this time I was starving. I wondered whether the new household arrangements ran to food and thought I could sniff something cooking once, but at seven her mum called up that she and the pillock were going down to their local for what she called a 'livener'.

Ella pushed open her bedroom door. 'Is there anything Holly and I can eat?' she called down.

I craned my head to see over the banisters. Ella's mum stood there in a short fake-fur coat. Her hair was in little blond corkscrews to her shoulders and at a glance, at a distance and if you were short-sighted, she could have been seventeen.

'You'll be lucky,' her mum said cheerfully. 'I'll bring you back a bag of chips if you're good.'

''S OK,' Ella said. She glanced at me. 'I expect Holly and I will go out for a burger or something.'

The pillock appeared and looked up at us. 'Ooh, I'd forgotten you were there,' he said, meaning me. 'You two girls must have had an awful lot to talk about. All personal and private, was it? No naughty-naughties, I hope.'

Ella just gave me a look and kicked the door shut without replying.

'Don't be like that!' he said. 'Tell us some naughties!'

Ella's mum gave a little shriek of laughter.

They went out and Ella looked at me despairingly. 'Oh, God,' she said.

I nodded slowly. 'Nightmare.'

'I haven't heard anything,' she said dully.

I knew what she meant. 'It's too soon yet, isn't it? They only wrote to him this week.'

'Yeah, but if someone wrote to you saying you were their daughter, wouldn't you just want to meet them straight away?'

I shrugged. 'Dunno,' I said. 'Maybe I'd want to think about it first. Sort of come to terms with it.'

'But he knew he had me!' she said. 'Not like you. Or him. That man – what's his name?'

'Ben,' I said.

'They would have written Wednesday, so he'd have got the letter on Thursday.'

'But it's only Saturday. And suppose he's away on his holidays? It's August, don't forget. And suppose they've got the wrong one? Suppose it's not him after all?'

She didn't speak for a long time, then she said, 'I hate it here. And I hate them.'

'I know,' I said.

It was my turn to pat her on the back.

We went out for a burger and saw Alex and a couple of his mates down the high street. I didn't fancy talking much, though, or really doing anything, so we didn't hang around. We went home and watched something mindless on TV instead.

At eleven the happy couple came back from the pub. Ella's mum went into the kitchen and he stood in the doorway of the sitting room, holding on to the door handle and swaying.

'Who wants a little nightcap?' he kept saying. 'Who wants a little nightcap with us? How about you, gorgeous Miss Holly Golightly?'

I decided to go home.

I didn't really want to, but there was something inside me which made me crave for the normality of my home and my own bedroom with its lilac duvet and new roller blinds and nice pine furniture. And what was the alternative? There wasn't one, apart from staying at Ella's or running away.

When I got back Mum must have been standing behind the door, waiting, because she opened it as soon as my hand touched the front gate.

'Have you been at Ella's?' she said. 'I was just about to ring her. I do wish you wouldn't walk home from there. Dad would have come and got you.'

I didn't say anything, just lifted my eyebrows meaningfully at this last sentence.

'I'm going to bed,' I said, going past her and straight up the stairs.

'We're going to Nan's tomorrow,' Mum said. 'You haven't forgotten, have you?'

'No,' I said, clipped and cold. I carried on walking and didn't even look at her.

'Dad's in the sitting room. Aren't you going to say goodnight?' she asked anxiously.

'Night!' I shouted and just carried on up.

I fell asleep quite quickly, but I woke after an hour and couldn't get back again; I just kept going over everything in long and painful detail in my head. I felt removed and distanced from Mum and it was a horrible, scary and alien feeling. We'd rowed in the past, of course, but even when we'd had a real go at each other, I'd known that it was just a blip, a temporary, tiny thing that could never alter the basic structure of our relationship.

This wasn't, though; this was a bomb, an earthquake, a destruction of the world as I'd known it. Everything I'd ever believed in was false.

I hated the man who'd done this, and I hated her as well. The only one I didn't hate was Dad, downstairs. I loved him – but in the end, who was he to me? Not my dad, that was for sure.

chapter twelve

The next day I sat in silence in the back of the car, looking out of the window.

'Nan's making us one of her chicken pies,' Mum said, glancing round at me. 'Home-made pastry and everything.'

I grunted something.

'I can't remember the last time I made pastry,' she went on brightly. 'A dying art, pastry-making is. Soon no one will be able to do it. It'll be like thatching.'

'But people are still learning to thatch,' Dad put in. 'It's one of those things that have started up again. People like houses with thatched roofs – it's something to do with the nostalgia kick.'

'I love thatched houses,' Mum said. 'And the more ratty the thatch, the better I like it. I think of all the little creatures who've made their homes inside it. Mice and birds and bats and … '

Off she went again, pretending she *cared* about things. Pretending she was a nice person who loved her family and would never deceive them. I gave a loud sigh and Dad looked at me in the driving mirror. 'What's up with you, love?'

Mum glanced over at me anxiously. I saw a nerve twitch at the corner of her mouth.

I shook my head. 'Nothing,' I muttered.

'Just a bit travel-sick, perhaps,' Mum said.

I didn't reply. How could this have happened to me? To *my* family? At school, I'd been one of the few to have an old-fashioned, quite boringly normal mum and dad, while others had single mums and dads or stepmums, dads, brothers and sisters coming out of their ears. I'd listened over the years, fascinated and appalled, to Ella's and everyone else's tales of stepparent horror, wondering how I'd managed to escape all these family ructions and even bizarrely wishing, sometimes, that I'd had some horror stories of my own to tell. I'd had no idea that I'd been living a horror story all along.

Now I knew that my family was just the same as everyone else's. Worse, because at least people like

Ella's mum were honest, shedding husbands and boyfriends and picking up with new ones quite openly, whereas my mum was deceitful, lying, *barbaric*, even – passing off another man's child on her husband without a qualm.

On the surface everything was the same. Underneath, though, the whole structure of my life had collapsed. I felt as if I had no control over my destiny any more; that anything could happen. Suppose he – Ben – put in a formal claim for me and took me away and made me live in America? I'd heard about tug-of-love babies and children – could you do that with teenagers?

What was going to happen? Was I going to tell anyone? *What was I going to do?*

'You've hardly touched your pie!' Nan said reproachfully. 'I thought it was your favourite.'

'It is,' I said guiltily. 'I'm just not very hungry.'

'I got up early to catch that chicken, too,' Grandad said, and I tried to smile.

We were sitting round the red Formica table in the kitchen of Nan and Grandad's bungalow. All around were the things I remembered from way back in my childhood: the green plastic clock with the broken

127

hand, the teddy-with-shield ornament I'd bought when I was three saying, 'Best Nan in the world', the postcards round the mirror, the plastic sheet with 'Everyday Phone Numbers' written on it, the dusty jug with an assortment of pens that didn't work.

'I hope you're not going on one of those silly slimming kicks,' Dad said. 'I can't bear those women who look like stick insects.'

'No, of course she wouldn't!' Mum said, ever-bright, ever-cheerful. 'Holly's much too sensible for that.'

'Are you looking forward to getting back to school?' Grandad asked.

I shook my head, pushing a sprout around my plate. 'I've quite enjoyed the freedom, actually. And I like having money to spend.'

'That job at the tea shop's been really good for you,' Nan said. 'I expect you'll work there every summer now, won't you?'

'Probably,' I agreed.

'Just tourists you get in there, is it?' Grandad asked.

I nodded. 'Mostly.'

'Tourists and your secret admirer!' Dad chipped in.

Opposite me, Mum dropped her fork on the floor.

'Who's that, then?' Nan asked.

'Someone's been sending our Holly presents,' Dad said. 'Scarf and flowers and something else – '

'Earrings,' I said.

'Well, I never!' Nan said. 'Were they nice?'

I nodded.

'How exciting! And you've no idea who they're from?'

It was a long while before I shook my head. Long enough for Mum to turn pale.

Later, me, Mum and Nan were sitting on the back porch watching Dad and Grandad cutting the hedge at the side of the garden.

I was looking at Dad and thinking it was just impossible to think he *wasn't* Dad when it suddenly struck me. If he wasn't Dad, then these two, his parents, weren't Nan and Grandad. They were total strangers. I didn't know why I hadn't thought of it before. And then, of course, Dad's brother and sister weren't my auntie and uncle, and my cousins weren't my cousins, and that new baby my cousin Sammy had just had, which everyone said was the spitting image of me, wasn't actually the slightest bit related.

I didn't have any relations except Mum. And I didn't want her.

'Your dad's putting on weight,' Nan said as we sat there.

'Who?' I said. I knew it wasn't really fair of me to bring this nice old lady who wasn't any relation of mine into it, but I was trying to get back at Mum and make her feel uneasy.

'Your dad,' Nan said, all unaware. 'He'll have to cut down on his portions of bread pudding. Still his favourite, is it?'

'Yes, he loves it,' Mum said. Her voice sounded tight and strained.

Nan went inside to make tea and while she was out of the way, Mum said something about it being hot. I didn't answer. *How could she have an affair with anyone? How could she deceive Dad?* I moved my chair so that it was slightly facing away from her. I hated her!

'I don't know what's the matter with you two today,' Nan said suddenly, coming out with a full tray of tea things. 'Not your usually bright and bubbly selves, are you?'

'Aren't we?' Mum said. 'Must be the weather. I was just saying to Holly that I keep coming over in big waves of heat.'

'Ah! Hot flushes,' Nan said, putting out cups. 'I remember them well.'

'I suppose that's what it is,' Mum said.

Was I going to tell anyone? What would happen if I told Dad?

Nan suddenly started laughing. 'You'll never guess what I've done,' she said. 'Put the hot water in this jug and – well, I don't use it very often. See for yourself.'

And she tipped up the jug to show us a small roll of banknotes floating in the hot water. 'It's my secret savings!' she said. 'I stash a little bit of money away every week out of the housekeeping – keep it in the jug.'

'What d'you keep it there for?' I asked.

Nan put her finger to her lips. 'Sssh. I like to have a little secret hoard,' she said. 'I put it in there so your Grandad won't find it.'

I knew she was only messing around and it wasn't serious, but I suddenly felt sick. Everyone had secrets from each other. No one was exactly as they seemed, and therefore the whole world was based on lies!

My eyes filled with tears. Abruptly, I got up and ran down to the bottom of the garden, past Dad and Grandad.

'Oh, dear,' I heard Nan say. 'What's up with our Holly?'

'Just her hormones, I expect,' Mum said.

chapter thirteen

'Your hat's drooping,' Ella said, reaching up to try and adjust the silly bit of white material on top of my head.

'Never mind that,' I said. '*I'm* drooping.'

It was coffee break and I'd just come down to the staffroom. We had five minutes together before Ella had to go back to serve in the shop.

'What happened yesterday, then?' she asked.

'Nothing. Went to Nan and Grandad's,' I said. 'Or should I say, went to Mr and Mrs Devine's. They're the parents of the man I live with. My mum's husband.'

Ella grinned at me. 'At least you've got them and they're nice.' She stood up and rustled her long skirt. 'If I find my dad, I might find I've got a nice nan and grandad too.' She started up the stairs. 'Talk to you properly at lunchtime,' she said.

I slumped, nibbling round the jam doughnut I'd bought downstairs. What was I going to do? How could I just go on at home pretending things were the same? What was going to happen?

At two o'clock that morning I'd woken up frightened – terrified – and for a while I hadn't been able to think why I was, just known that there was a knot of terror in the pit of my stomach. Then I'd remembered why it was there, and I'd twisted and turned and lain in a hundred different positions to try and soothe it away, but in the end I'd had to go downstairs and get a hot-water bottle. Once I had that, I'd screwed myself up into a foetal position, bottle on my tummy, and tried to rock myself to sleep. Talk about pathetic – I only just managed to stop myself from sucking my thumb.

It had been ages before I'd been able to get off again: I'd watched the silvery laser arms of my bedside clock gently touch all the way round the clock face at least three times. Mum was awake, too, and I was nastily pleased about that. I heard her go into the bathroom a couple of times and then, around four, go down to the kitchen and make a cup of tea. At any other time, if I'd heard her down there in the night, I would have gone to see if she was all right and we might have shared a cuppa and a biscuit – but not now. All that was finished.

It was Mrs Potter's day off so we weren't too rushed that morning. We had as many customers, but we just didn't bother quite as much with them – like, we didn't rush up the moment they arrived to greet them, or clear the tables quite as readily. Cody tried to keep us up to scratch, but we didn't work the same for him.

At lunchtime Ella rang the helpline again.

'They said they'd ring you if they heard anything,' I reminded her as she dialled.

'They're busy people,' she said. 'They might not have had time. I'll just save them the phone call.'

She got through to Maureen and I saw her face drop. 'Nothing? Nothing at all? Why d'you think that is?'

Ella beckoned me to come nearer and I squashed myself by the phone. 'The person at the garage could be away – or maybe he just hasn't bothered to respond,' I heard Maureen say.

'Could you tell me where the garage is?' Ella asked. She put her hand over the mouthpiece. 'We could go there,' she mouthed to me.

'I'm afraid we can't tell you that. You see, some people want to stay missing and we have to respect their wishes.'

'D'you think *he* wants to stay missing?' Ella asked anxiously.

'It's too soon to say,' Maureen said. 'And don't forget, we might not even have the right man. The only information we've had is a call from someone saying that a man of the same name works at his garage.'

'Suppose it's not him, then? What happens next?'

'We'll just carry on looking. There are other things we can try – other places we can look for him. Try not to worry.'

Ella said thanks and sorry to have troubled her and then put the phone down and stared at me. 'They've got the right bloke – bet it *is* him in the garage,' she said. 'I've just got a feeling about it.'

I didn't know what to say.

'It's him but he's got another family now and he just couldn't care less about me.'

'Don't be daft! Why have you suddenly started thinking that? You've been listening to the pillock, haven't you?'

She shook her head. 'It's just common sense. I've got to face it. He would have found some way to get in touch if he wanted to. If he really cared about me.'

I shrugged. 'Maybe he's somewhere abroad – '

'Oh, yeah. Abroad somewhere you can't send letters from. Like, he's in the middle of the jungle or something and he's been there for fourteen years and never seen a post office.'

As I grinned, she added, 'I'm beginning to wish I hadn't started looking.'

'How's that?'

'Well, all the time I wasn't looking for him I could pretend how it would be if I ever found him. But if I do actually find him and he doesn't want me, then that's much worse … '

I made sympathetic noises. I didn't know what else I could do.

Cody shouted down to us that we were three minutes late getting back from lunch and what did we think this was, a place of work or a rest home, so we went up and I took over from Mandy on section three.

The first customer I saw was *him*, Ben, sitting there with his long legs stretched out into the aisle and an Earl Grey tea in front of him.

My legs automatically went into wobble mode and

I turned to go back downstairs. Cody was standing at the top of them barring my way, though, so there was nothing for it but to walk up to his table and face him.

'What are you doing here?' I asked coldly.

He gave a small smile, spread his hands. 'Sorry,' he said. 'Couldn't resist it. I go back to the States on Wednesday morning so this is my last time. Positively my last visit. After Thursday you can relax.'

'Why did you come?' I asked. 'I wish you hadn't.'

'Sorry,' he said again. 'I know you do.'

'You've made my life … ' I shrugged; *hell* didn't seem strong enough. There wasn't a word to say how much he'd wrecked things. 'My life was quite OK before – the only thing I had to worry about was whether my jeans were the right make. Now it's a mess.'

'I can only imagine,' he said. 'And for that I'm profoundly sorry. Look, can you just sit down with me for ten minutes – '

'No!'

'Five minutes, then? Two minutes? Two minutes is all I ask. I just want to talk to you. Tell you how it was between your mom and me.'

I glanced towards Cody. 'I don't want to hear things like that.'

'I think it would help. I'd just like to clear a few things up before I go back. I don't want to go off leaving your life in complete chaos. I'd feel better if you were straight on just a couple of things. *Please*. If you could bear it.'

I wanted to say no, but I found myself walking up to Cody, saying there was a bit of an emergency and asking if I could have five minutes with a customer because of some quite exceptional circumstances. I said I'd work right though the afternoon without a break to make up for it. Cody, very intrigued, said OK.

I sat down opposite him. 'Five minutes, and then you've got to go,' I said. 'Do you promise?'

'Promise.' He stared at me. 'You believe me now, don't you? Believe that what I said is true.'

I set my lips stubbornly. He wasn't going to get anything out of me. I wasn't going to confirm or deny a thing.

'You don't have to say, I can see that you do. Did you ask your mom?'

I looked out of the window.

'Yes, I can guess that you did. And I'm pretty sure she would have denied it. So I guess that you found some other sort of evidence, right?'

138

I still stared, watching the doodles swarming across the street.

'Look, I want you to tell her from me that I won't make any demands, I won't rock the boat, I won't tell your dad – Gordon, isn't it? – and I won't do anything that will upset either of you.'

'You've already done that.'

'All I want is – well, I don't even allow myself to pretend that you're ever going to acknowledge me, but it would be fantastic if I could possibly see you next time I'm over here. You don't have to look like that, it won't be for another year. And if ever you could bring yourself to visit with me in the States then that would be … ' His eyes lit up and I didn't know *what* it would be because the words got choked up in his throat.

'Visit you!' I said. 'I wouldn't visit you if you were the other side of the street. And how am I supposed to *visit* you without telling my dad?'

He looked at me pleadingly and shrugged. I glanced away. 'You said you were going to explain about you and Mum.'

'Yes. I just wanted to tell you that it wasn't a sordid sort of thing. We thought we loved each other.'

I winced. 'And what about my dad? Where did he come into all this?'

'He was working late hours – until ten at night sometimes. Your mom was young and lively and she was feeling neglected.'

'So?'

'Look, I'm going to talk to you as an adult, Holly. OK?'

'OK,' I muttered. I hoped he wasn't going to mention sex. The act. I didn't want to hear where I'd been conceived or anything.

'She and I just used to go out for a drink occasionally. And as we got to know each other and made each other laugh and so on, the more we liked each other. And then the inevitable happened.'

I was silent.

'And then – well, I knew I had this job in the States coming up, and I wanted your mom to come with me. She just couldn't decide what to do. She didn't want to hurt your dad and she didn't want to move away from her home and friends, either. We had about two months of horrible indecision where neither of us knew what to do for the best, and then we had a weekend away together. In March 1984, that was. The following month she told me she couldn't come away with me and so it had to be all over between us. I went abroad at the end of April.'

'And that was that?'

He nodded. 'I wrote to her several times but she never replied. And then – well, life goes on, doesn't it? Eventually I started dating other women and then I met Jennie and we married about twelve years ago. I've never forgotten your mom, though. I really loved her.'

'So you didn't think … she never told you she was pregnant?'

He shook his head. 'I never had the slightest idea. She never told me and it certainly didn't occur to me. I guess she did what she thought was best for you, Holly.'

'What was easiest for her, you mean,' I said bitterly.

'No,' he said. 'Your mom's a good woman. She put you first.'

'Huh!' I said bitterly.

'Holly, she's brought you up well and the last thing I want to do is drive some sort of wedge between you.'

'Consider it driven,' I said.

'For Christ's sake!' He rubbed his hand through his hair vigorously. 'Look, talk to her about it. Ask her what happened. *Please*.'

'I don't want to know what happened.'

'It might help you understand,' he said.

At the back of the shop, I saw Cody look at me and pointedly tap his watch. 'I've got to get back to work,' I said. 'And you promised you'd go after five minutes.'

'OK.' He managed to smile but it looked like an effort. 'Thanks for talking to me.' He stretched out his right hand as if he wanted to grasp my shoulder, but I stepped back from him and his hand fell. He reached into his pocket for a card. 'This is my address,' he said. 'If – one day – you could bring yourself to contact me, that would be brilliant. And if you're ever in any trouble … '

'Don't hold your breath,' I said.

'Pardon me?'

'Oh, it's just an expression we have,' I said, taking the card.

'Don't throw it away, will you?'

I shook my head. 'No. Might even … ' I shrugged. I didn't know.

I watched him leave the shop and walk down the street. Bewilderingly – how odd is this? – I found that I didn't hate him.

chapter fourteen

'He came in the shop today,' was the first thing I said. When I got in from work, Mum had been sitting at the kitchen table smoking, just slumped there, staring at nothing. I think it was the first time I'd ever come in and she hadn't rushed to get me a drink or at least asked me if I'd had a nice day or anything.

When I said that, she looked up at me and gasped. 'No!' she said, and then immediately started crying, putting her head down on the table and rocking backwards and forwards.

I didn't know what to do. I'd hardly ever seen Mum crying before, and never in such a hopeless, forlorn way. It took everything in me not to go and sit next to her and put my arm round her. It took a *huge* effort not to start crying myself.

'What does he want?' she said, looking up at me with a distorted, wet face. '*What does he want?*'

'Not much,' I said. 'I mean, he doesn't want to take me away or anything.'

'What does he want, then? What's he doing it for?'

'He just wants it acknowledged, really. He wants you – us – to admit that he's my father.'

'I can't do that!'

'But he is, isn't he?' I said. 'At least admit it to me, Mum. Don't you think I've got the right to know?'

She broke into fresh tears. I sat there for a while just looking at her, hating her, and then I pushed the tea towel along the table so she could wipe her eyes.

'He is, isn't he?' I said again.

After a long while she nodded. 'I think he may be. I think he probably is.'

I heaved a great sigh. 'There. Now I know.' It was a bit of an anticlimax really, because I think I'd known all along. From the first time he'd said it. People don't go round making up things like that, do they?

'But I've never been absolutely sure,' she added. She rubbed her hand across her face, leaving a streak of mascara across her cheek. 'I'll tell you … ' she said.

I pulled out a chair and sat opposite her. I felt

strangely cold and alien – and very grown-up. I felt like I'd matured about ten years during the day.

'I wasn't getting on very well with your dad – '

'Which dad?' I couldn't resist asking.

'With … with Gordon,' she said. 'We were just going through a bit of a bad patch. Like all relationships do.'

I stared at her stonily.

'I met Ben and went out with him a few times and we got on very well. We started an affair.' She glanced at me. 'And you don't have to look at me like that. I know it's wrong, but not many people go through life being totally faithful to one person. I know it's no excuse but – ' she looked at me sadly – 'we're all human, you know. We've all got failings. Even mums and dads.'

'It wasn't just that, though,' I said bitterly. 'You passed off someone else's baby! You pretended I was Dad – was Gordon's child!'

'I know,' Mum said. 'Wait. Just hear me out.' She wiped her eyes again on the tea towel. 'After we'd been seeing each other – '

'Not just seeing!' I put in.

Mum sighed. 'After we'd been having an affair for several months, Ben got the opportunity to take this really good job in the States. It was something he'd been waiting for. He asked me to go there with him, and I had to decide what to do. I thought about it, talked to your gran and even went to a counsellor about it, and in the end decided that I wanted to stay here. That I really did love your – love Gordon. I decided that I'd make a real effort with my marriage. I spoke to Dad – I didn't tell him about Ben, though – and we went for marriage guidance and gradually got back on the even keel we'd been on previously.'

'And then?'

'And then halfway through all this, through the marriage guidance and so on, I found that I was pregnant.' She glanced at me again, 'And before you ask – I was overjoyed. I was thirty-four then and in those days it was quite late for a first baby, and I'd begun to think I couldn't have one.' She slid her hand along the table towards me, but I put my own out of the way in my lap.

'Gordon was overjoyed, too. He looked upon it as the final seal on the renewal of our marriage. We even went and retook our wedding vows.' She smiled a little. 'How schmaltzy is that!'

'But you must have thought – '

'I knew, of course, that there was a chance it could

have been Ben's baby, but I immediately squashed that thought down. Never allowed myself to dwell on it.'

'But what about when I was born?'

'When you were born – oh, it was sheer joy! Having a baby was the most blissful thing for us and we loved every moment of it. We boasted about you to everyone and took masses of photos and spoilt you rotten. Gordon was so good a dad that to have even suggested to him that you might not be his child would have been ... ' She shook her head. 'Well, it would have killed him.'

'But I don't even look like him!'

'Loads of children don't look like their parents,' Mum said. She added in a low voice, 'Though I must admit when I noticed you had Ben's funny eye – '

'And his colouring and height.'

There was a long silence, then Mum said, 'I just did what I thought was the best thing at the time.'

'Best for you.'

'Best for all of us. And I thought I'd got away with it.' She paused and tried to reach out and touch me. 'Do you think you can ever forgive me, Holly?'

'I don't know,' I said. 'Shouldn't think so.'

'You're the most important person in my life.' Her voice went husky as if she was going to start crying again. 'I can't imagine life without you. I can't bear it if you don't forgive me.'

Tears sprang into my own eyes but I didn't want her to see them so I got up and looked out of the window. 'I don't know,' I said again.

'If you could just forget this ever happened … '

'I can't do that,' I said. 'And even if I could, other people know now. I've told Alex about it. And Ella.'

Mum gave a low moan.

'You'll have to tell him, Mum,' I said. 'You'll have to tell Dad. Gordon.'

'I can't!'

'He's got to know. It's not fair.'

'It'll kill him,' she said dully.

'If you don't tell him, I will,' I said, though I was lying. I couldn't have told him myself in a hundred years.

Mum got on with a meal and I went up and lay on my bed. It had been a weird day. First of all I'd found that I didn't hate Ben. And now it seemed that I didn't hate Mum either. It had something to do with the shock having retreated a bit, and then with having everything explained, and also something to do with what Mum had said about only being human. If I stopped thinking of Mum as *Mum*, and started thinking of her as a person, it was easier. I knew that Ella still somehow managed to love her mum. She thought she was a slapper and gullible and pathetic when it came to men, but she still loved her.

But even if I did still love Mum and eventually forgave her, my life was an enormous, horrible mess. Suppose when Dad found out he chucked me out? Chucked Mum out? Suppose he told Nan and Grandad? What would everyone say?

I got under the duvet and I rolled into as small a ball as I could. Whatever happened, Dad was going to have to know because I couldn't stand to live with him – or with us as a family – until he did.

chapter fifteen

I hardly ate two mouthfuls of supper. And Mum didn't either. The only one to eat was Dad, who tucked into a full plate of spaghetti not knowing he had a huge hatchet poised over his head.

We went into the sitting room and Dad put the TV on. I didn't watch the screen, just sat and stared at Mum, waiting to see what she was going to do. My stomach was still knotted and the smell of Bolognese sauce in the air was making me feel sick.

Mum was white and looked droopy around the eyes, a nerve ticking away at the side of her face. I wanted to say, *Sit down, Mum, and I'll make you a cup of tea*, or *Don't worry, Mum. You don't have to say anything after all.* I thought how lovely it would be to say that to her and to see her face clear and lighten.

I couldn't do that, though. I knew it wouldn't be right. It would just leave things hanging in the air over us all. I needed to get things out in the open.

We sat through a whole episode of *EastEnders* and no one said anything. At the end of it as the music was pumping out, Dad said, quite chattily, 'Do I detect a chill in the air? Have you two had words?'

I didn't say anything, just got up and turned off the TV and he looked at me, surprised. 'What's up, then?'

'Mum's got something to tell you,' I said. I looked at her. 'Do you want me to go upstairs?'

Mum shook her head and started crying, and I started crying as well, while Dad sat there looking from one to the other of us as if we'd gone completely off our heads. 'What on earth is it? What … this isn't just some tiff, is it? This is more than that.'

I shook my head and tears flicked off my face on to my clenched hands. 'It's much worse,' I said.

'I get it. I see,' he said sternly. He cleared his throat. 'I take it that you're pregnant, are you, Holly?'

'No!' I said, but at that moment I wouldn't have minded that. Even being pregnant with ginger twins seemed preferable to what was actually happening.

'It's about me,' Mum said.

'What … what – are you ill or something?

Seriously ill? For God's sake tell me and stop all this carrying on.'

'OK, OK,' Mum said. She got up, took a tissue from the box on the table and blew her nose. She took a deep breath and then she said, 'I would have done anything to save you from this, Gordon, but circumstances have changed and I now think … that is, Holly does … that you should know.'

Dad frowned. 'I still don't know what the bloody hell you're talking about. Please make yourself clear.'

Mum took another breath in. 'You see, years ago, I had an affair.'

Dad stiffened, but didn't say anything.

'You and I weren't getting on too well at the time,' she said, 'although I'm not trying to justify myself by saying that. It – the affair – was quite a temporary thing. Altogether it lasted about five months, and then the person concerned went abroad and went out of my life.'

Dad stood up suddenly, put his hands in his pockets, went to the window and stared out. I couldn't bear to look at him in case he was crying. 'Is that it?' he asked in a clipped voice.

'No.' Mum said. 'I'm afraid … I'm very much afraid that it gets worse than that.'

I pulled my legs up to my body, shut my eyes, put my head between my knees and hugged myself tightly, waiting …

'You see, I got pregnant and I wasn't completely sure whose baby it was. Yours or his. And I'm afraid … I just let it be thought that it – that Holly – was yours.'

Dad was still silent, but he was making little puffing sounds under his breath, like he was having difficulty breathing. I started worrying what would happen if he had a heart attack. If he did, it would be my fault, because I'd made Mum tell him.

'You see, I've never been really sure. Even now I don't know for definite,' Mum went on in a faraway voice. 'Even when I saw things in Holly that I thought might have … come from him, it made so much more sense to keep quiet. We've always been happy together, as a family. I didn't want anything to change that. Despite what had happened, I realised that I loved you – and I knew you loved us. I just couldn't bring myself to destroy all that we had.'

There was a long, long silence and I just stayed as I was, hugged in tightly, pretending it wasn't happening, and then I heard a little choking noise and when I looked up Dad was doubled up with his head bowed low, crying. Mum was watching him with a look of such misery and longing on her face, and I knew she desperately wanted to go and comfort him but didn't dare.

I jumped up, ran over and tried to put my arms round him. 'We do still both love you!' I said.

He wrenched away from me, as if ashamed to let me see him crying. 'Why did you have to tell me now?'

Mum said, 'Because he ... because the man who may be Holly's father ... came back here and saw Holly and put two and two together.'

'Those presents?' Dad asked.

'That's right. I didn't know they were from him ... not until I went off with Holly to meet him that time. And then of course I tried to stop her from having anything to do with him.'

Dad started walking up and down the sitting room, taking deep breaths to try and stop himself from crying. I watched him and thought I'd never seen such an awful sight in my life. Mum crying was one thing, *him* crying was quite another.

'Say something. Say something!' I begged. 'You do still want to be my dad, don't you?'

There was about another two minutes when he just

paced up and down, and then he said, 'I knew. I suspected.'

Neither Mum nor I said anything and he said again, 'I knew.'

'Knew what?' Mum said, astonished. 'How did you know?'

'D'you think I'm stupid? I knew we were going through a dodgy patch. I guessed you were seeing someone else. And then when you got pregnant I knew there was a fair chance that the baby wasn't mine.'

'How?'

'Because I've never been one hundred per cent sure that I could have children.' He blew his nose and seemed to pull himself together. He was on to facts now and he was better at facts than emotions. 'I had mumps as a teenager, and that sometimes reduces your fertility. I never told you about that before we got married, though, because I knew how much you wanted a baby. So you see, I can be capable of deception, too.'

Mum didn't say anything. I guess she was trying to take it all in.

'Once – when we lived in the other house – you got a letter. An airmail letter. You tried to pretend it was from an old aunt or something but I knew from the way you took it and hid it away that it was from some-one important, about something secret. I looked everywhere for that letter, but I never found it.'

He glanced at me. 'And then as Holly grew … ' His voice went husky again. ' … grew into a lovely young lady, I knew she wasn't mine. She was tall and fair and beautiful and I was none of those things.'

'Dad!' I implored him.

'But I went along with the game, just like you did. I couldn't do anything else.' He paused and blew his nose again 'So what do you want to do now?'

Mum shook her head. 'I don't want to do anything,' she said. 'Nothing! I want things to stay exactly as they are. I just wanted you to know the truth.' She glanced at me. '*Holly* wanted you to know the truth. I think … I believe you're her father. Not biologically, maybe, but in terms of care and love and trust and everything else. We've brought her up together, we've been a family, and no one can change that now. It's just whether you can forgive me or not.'

Dad looked at me. 'Do you want to change any-thing, Holly? Do you … do you want to go and live with this man?'

I started blubbing again so that I could hardly speak. 'Of course I don't!'

There was a long silence. 'Well, then,' Dad said, and he wiped his eyes on his sleeve. 'Come here, then, love.'

As he said it, Mum said it as well, but it was Dad I went to.

He put his arms round me and I leaned hard on his shoulder and pressed my face into his jumper. I couldn't speak. I wanted to ask him if he still loved me now that he knew I wasn't his and stuff like that, but I couldn't begin to put those sorts of things into words.

Out in the hall, the phone began to ring. We all ignored it, but it rang and rang and in the end went on to the answerphone.

'Holly!' I heard Ella screech. 'Guess what?'

In the sitting room we were frozen like shop-window dummies, just listening.

'Holly! Are you there? Guess what?' Ella said again. Then she said, 'My dad got in touch! He rang the helpline. It was him working at that person's garage! Isn't it brilliant? I can't believe it!' She paused for breath and then she said, 'Ring me when you get in and I'll tell you all about it. He lives in Essex and he wants to meet me! I can't believe it!' Another pause and she added, slightly hesitantly, 'I hope everything's all right. Goodbye.'

After a moment Dad sighed. 'That's good,' he said, nodding his head towards the phone.

'Yes,' I said. I suddenly felt unbearably tired. As if I'd fall down if I didn't sit down. I couldn't face sitting with Mum, though. Not yet.

I gave Dad a bit of a smile, just to let him know I was all right, and went out of the room and upstairs to my bedroom. I felt I wanted to cry for a long time and then sleep for a year.

chapter sixteen

On Wednesday morning I stood in the flight departures hall, looking around me. For once the shops and the snazzy-looking coffee bars didn't attract me, because I was searching for something else. Someone else.

All was quiet at home. Sort of the lull after the storm. Mum and Dad both looked drawn and ill at ease and neither of them was eating or – judging from the cups of tea being made in the night – sleeping much, either. They were speaking to each other, though, and soon, maybe, the number of years they'd been together would kind of drag them through and back to normality. I hoped I'd be able to get back to normality, too. Things had changed and shifted and I didn't feel the same about certain things but I thought that I could, just about, learn to adjust. My life had moved into a different gear, I just had to try to move with it.

'We are now boarding for flight V101 to San Francisco,' the tannoy announced. 'Will passengers please go to Gate 54.'

I knew he might be on this flight, and I stopped in my tracks. I knew you couldn't go to the flight gates or even into the departure lounge unless you were a passenger, and if this was his flight he was probably through there now and just about to board. I'd been about to go to the Virgin counter and ask if they had a passenger named Ben Simmons, but now I mentally shrugged and turned in the direction of the departure lounge.

Why had I come? I didn't exactly know. It had been more a question of waking in the morning and thinking to myself that I might as well, and ringing Mrs Potter at the shop, and then ringing Heathrow to find out times of possible flights. I'd missed two of them by the time I got there, but there were two more that morning, so I'd decided to leave it to fate. If I got there and saw him, OK. If I didn't, then that was fairly OK too.

When I got to the wide channel which led to the

departure lounge, an Asian family were just going through with a whole lot of bags, babies and grannies in bright saris. I stood at the head of the slope and tried to look past them, but beyond where the staff checked the boarding cards there were screens which prevented you from seeing further in.

If he was booked on the Virgin flight, he was somewhere in there and I'd missed him. But there was a BA flight in an hour's time and he might be on that. I stood there, undecided, not knowing whether to go and check with the other airline or wait there or what.

And then, as I was hesitating, I saw him: a tall, fair man in a navy-blue suit, an overnight bag over his shoulder, going through the customs desk.

'Hey!' I started down the slope but he didn't turn. He showed the man his passport and went through into no man's land.

'Hey!' I said again. 'Hello!'

Just as he reached the screens he turned and saw me. He looked bewildered at first, then amazed, then delighted. I thought what a strange feeling it was: having the power to make someone be all those things.

Three businessmen came behind him, pressing him through to the x-ray machines, so I couldn't go to him and he couldn't come to me and that was just as well, because I wouldn't have wanted any big hugging and kissing scene.

We saw each other, and we waved, and that was enough.

He's my father. I know that one day I'll see him again.

epilogue

Nearly a year's gone by since the day I went to the airport. I'm in sixth form now and I've just done my first year exams. They weren't a complete disaster, so I hope I'll be going to university next year.

Mum and Dad are sort of back on an even keel. The thing that helped, strangely enough, was that Dad had had mumps. He said he should have told Mum about that before they got married, knowing how much she wanted children. He told her that because he'd been capable of deceit, he felt more able to forgive her.

I guess I've forgiven her too. The thing she did was against Dad, so if he can forgive her it wouldn't be right for me not to. Anyway, it doesn't take much to forgive your mum, I've discovered, because you want her there so much. The thought of being alienated from her, of not having her in my life, is too terrible to think about, whatever she's done. I love her just as much, although I may not feel the same about her. I realise now that that's not altogether a bad thing, though, and that as you go through life your relationships change and adjust and sometimes find a new level.

I love Dad just as much, too – more, probably. And he really will always be my dad, no matter what Ben or anyone else says. That part hasn't changed.

Last year, after it happened, we were all a bit awkward with each other. A bit stiff and starchy and ultra-polite around the house. But now things are almost back to normal. Like, I can have a row with Mum without being tempted to call her names and Dad can say things like, 'Look, I'm your father and if I want you in at a certain time … ' without being self-conscious about it or making me squirm inside.

And today I'm at the airport again and I'm flying to San Francisco so I'm dead excited. Ben and Jennie are meeting me there to take me to their home in Monterey. Just for two weeks, of course, because my home, and my mum and dad are here …

National Missing Persons Helpline is a charity
(Reg No 1020419) that tries to contact missing
people and offers advice and support for
their families as they wait for news.
They run a Helpline especially for young
people who have run away, enabling
them to send a message to their family or
carer and to receive advice and help:

Message Home Helpline 0800 700 740

Other titles by the same author

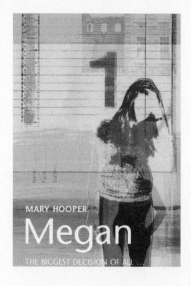

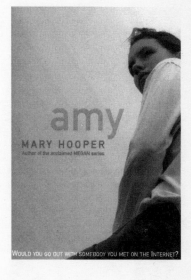

More great fiction from Bloomsbury

CATHERINE MACPHAIL

DARK WATERS

By the author of **MISSING**

Coraline

Neil Gaiman

'It is a masterpiece' **Terry Pratchett**

the named

marianne curley